THE
W·O·R·M
TUNNEL

A FINNEGAN ZWAKE MYSTERY

MICHAEL DAHL

AN ARCHWAY PAPERBACK
Published by POCKET BOOKS

New York   London   Toronto   Sydney   Singapore

This book is a work of fiction. Names, characters, places and inci-
dents are products of the author's imagination or are used fictious-
ly. Any resemblance to actual events or locales or persons, living or
dead, is entirely coincidental.

AN ARCHWAY PAPERBACK *Original*

An Archway Paperback published by
POCKET BOOKS, a division of Simon & Schuster Inc.
1230 Avenue of the Americas, New York, NY 10020

Copyright © 1999 by Michael Dahl

ISBN: 0-671-03270-4

First Archway Paperback printing October 1999

10 9 8 7 6 5 4 3

AN ARCHWAY PAPERBACK and colophon are
registered trademarks of Simon & Schuster Inc.

Front cover illustration by Lisa Falkenstern

Printed in the U.S.A.

IL 7+

"Hurry," I said. "The pool is getting higher."

Nixon nodded, his hair dripping, and followed me, limping, down the tunnel. The tunnel grew darker, but Nixon had a small flashlight hooked to his belt. Thunder rumbled above us. The sloping floor seemed to be climbing, but the water level was climbing too. In a few minutes the water had reached our knees.

"Now where do we go?" I said. The tunnel ended with three separate portholes, or mouths, leading out of it. "Which one do we take?"

"Look out!" shouted Nixon. I turned and saw a crocodile paddling along the surface of the water.

**BE SURE TO READ EVERY
FINNEGAN ZWAKE MYSTERY:**

THE HORIZONTAL MAN
THE WORM TUNNEL
THE RUBY RAVEN*

*coming soon

AVAILABLE FROM POCKET BOOKS

To Mom and Dad

THE
W·O·R·M
TUNNEL

1
The Disappearing Chinese Cowboy

"He's not real," said Uncle Stoppard. "He's just a mirage."

"Mirage or not," said Jared Lemon-Olsen, "we're not stopping to pick him up. Hitchhikers are dangerous. Especially in Mexico."

"We're not in Mexico anymore," I pointed out. "This is Agualar."

"The answer is still no," said Jared. "While I'm driving, I make the decisions."

We had crossed the Mexican-Agualaran border half an hour ago. Jared Lemon-Olsen, Uncle Stoppard's cop buddy, had insisted on driving the rental car ever since our plane landed in Mexico City, which was about nine hours ago. The hot afternoon sun beat down on the flat black highway and on the flat brown desert that surrounded us. A mile ahead lay a bright wall of gold.

"What is that?" Jared pointed. "Another mirage?"

Uncle Stoppard leaned over from the backseat. "That, my friend, is the beginning of the real Agualar. *La selva del oro.* The Gold Forest."

"Cactus," I said.

The *oro*, or gold, was miles and miles of Golden Finger cacti. Each cactus stood fifteen feet tall, thick, rounded branches shaped like fat golden fingers reached up to the cloudless sky. A million needles poked out of each wrinkly cactus skin. That's what I had read in the *Manual del Agualar,* or *Guide to Agualar,* that Uncle Stoppard had bought me at the airport. And I had had plenty of time to read.

"Those cacti are a national treasure," said Uncle Stoppard. "It's against the law to deface them or dig them up."

"Who would want to dig up a cactus?" I said.

"Gardeners, landscapers, real-estate developers. Cactus rustling is big business."

Jared whistled through his yellow mustache. "Interesting country," he said. "Kill the tourists, but don't touch the plants."

"It's a five-thousand-dollar fine if you do," said Uncle Stoppard. "Touch the plants, I mean."

Uncle Stoppard must had read about that in his own copy of the *Manual.*

Alongside the highway, still ahead of us, but still far from the beginning of the golden cactus fields, stood a man. Uncle Stoppard thought it was a mirage. I said it was a man. I was sitting in the passenger seat, so I had a clear view of the hitchhiker. As soon as I could see the figure, standing there in the distance, I asked Jared to stop for him. It must have been a hundred degrees out there in the sun. The desert was full of burning, snaky waves of hot air. You could see the highway ahead of us wiggling in the heat, slithering like a giant black snake. The air-conditioning in our rental car might not be working, but at least we had a breeze from the open windows.

"Do you know how many tourists get killed by hitchhikers each year?" asked Jared. "Especially in Mexi—uh, in Central America?"

"How many?" said Uncle Stoppard. He stretched out in the backseat and shifted his baseball cap to shade his sunglasses.

"At least forty tourists are killed each year. That's more than three a month," said Jared. "And I don't want us to become this month's statistics."

"Don't you think he's thirsty?" I asked.

"Mirages don't get thirsty," said Uncle Stoppard. "They're illusions."

"That guy is not an illusion."

"Hand me another can of pop, Finn," said Uncle Stoppard.

"And each day there are six to seven hijackings," Jared said. "Each day!"

I'm sure Jared was right. And I'm sure he didn't get his information out of a handbook. After all, he was a cop. That was one of the reasons Uncle Stoppard thought it was a good idea for Jared to come with us on our trip to Agualar. Jared was smart and strong and good in emergencies. But he wasn't the only person on this trip who knew about death and killers and stuff. Everyone in my family is an expert on dead things.

One of my grandmothers, for instance, was a paleontologist and collected fossils for museums. My other grandmother was a spook. You know, a spy with the CIA. Her husband, my grandfather, worked in the dead letter department of the Tombstone, Arizona, post office. Dad's favorite band is the Grateful Dead. Mom's favorite writer is Robert Graves. Both my parents were archeologists. I mean, *are* archeologists. I mean, *both*. Both are both. As of this moment they're alive but considered legally dead, since they disappeared over seven years ago while searching for Tquuli the Haunted City tucked somewhere among the frozen volcano-cones of Iceland. How do I know they're alive? If there's one thing people in our family know, it's if something is dead or not.

My name is Finnegan Zwake. My uncle Stoppard calls me Finn. I'm living with him back in Minneapolis until my parents come back. To look at us, you'd never guess we were related. Uncle Stoppard is tall and muscular with wavy red hair, crinkly green eyes, and a big nose (he calls it *aquiline*). I am not tall or muscular, have light-brown hair, pale skin, and freckles. Uncle Stoppard says I have a *mochaccino* crop, *java* eyes, and a *triple-latte* complexion with *nutmeg sprinkles*. Uncle Stoppard likes drinking coffee. He also likes using unusual words.

The only thing we share is our glasses. I mean, we both *wear* glasses. And, of course, we share the family fondness for dead things: I like ghost stories and Uncle Stop writes murder mysteries. We've been living together a little more than seven years now, and I guess I've gotten used to living in his apartment building in south Minneapolis. I don't think about my parents as much as I used to. Now I only think about them a couple times a day.

A few months ago I saw my first dead body. In the basement of our apartment building. In our storage locker. It was the same storage locker that held Mayan gold my parents discovered down in an archeological dig in Agualar. The same burning, boiling Agualar that we were now driving through with all our windows open.

Not all of Agualar is a desert. After we pass through *la selva del oro*, the golden cactus forest, I knew the highway would dip and twist down toward the Gulf of Mexico, and we'd be deep in a tropical jungle full of parrots and snakes and panthers. That's where my parents had their dig, near the eastern coast of Agualar. And that's exactly where Uncle Stop and Jared and I were heading.

Seven years ago my parents had been hired by the wealthy Ackerberg Institute to dig in Agualar. I was only six at the time. My parents were very good at digging holes. Truckloads of gold artifacts made by the ancient Maya people were dug up by my parents, dusted off, cleaned up, recorded, photographed, and packed into special protective boxes. But then a giant tropical storm had threatened the coast of Agualar, Hurricane Midge. My parents and I, along with all the other workers, were forced to evacuate the campsite. Dad and Mom rushed back to Minneapolis carrying all their treasure with them. They left the gold in Uncle Stoppard's care, along with their other treasure—me—and then flew off on another expedition to Iceland. They told Uncle Stoppard that they were worried about bringing me with them because of the extreme temperature shift from Agualar to Iceland. As if living in Minneapolis doesn't prepare you for extreme temperature shifts!

Uncle Stoppard is a great guy, but he isn't the most organized person in the world. It wasn't until we discovered the dead body that Uncle Stop remembered the

Mayan stuff in his storage room. Seven years *after* my parents had left it with him. Some spooky guys from the Ackerberg Institute finally showed up and claimed it. They wore black suits, black ties, and black leather gloves. And sunglasses. And they came at night. They took all the gold, but we kept my father's journals.

Funny thing about those journals. A few weeks ago, back in Minneapolis, Uncle Stoppard was reading one of the journals during our weekly Friday night pizza dinner. I was pulling the pepperoni circles off my slice and building them into a tower.

"Finn," he said to me. "Are you learning Spanish in school?"

"Uh, no. This year I picked science fiction and bowling for my electives."

"Bowling?"

"It's an Olympic sport, you know."

"What are you doing with that pepperoni?"

"It's the Leaning Tower of Pizza."

Uncle Stoppard stared at me and crinkled up his cucumber-green eyes. "I wonder if Pablo is home," he said.

Pablo de Soto was our neighbor and lived in the apartment just across the landing from ours. After dinner we walked over, and Pablo answered his door with a watering can in his hand. His apartment is a jungle. No parrots or panthers, just droopy plants in pots.

"Do me a favor, Pablo. Tell me what this says." Uncle Stoppard handed him Dad's journal.

Pablo gave Uncle Stoppard a puzzled look. "All right," he said, setting his watering can on a small table and squinting at the journal.

"Sorry, Stoppard," he said. "I can't help you."

"Oh, okay," said Uncle Stoppard. "Well, I didn't mean to bother you. I shouldn't have assumed you knew Spanish."

"I do know Spanish," Pablo said. "But this isn't Spanish. It's Portuguese."

Why would Dad write some entries in Portuguese?

"You sure?" asked Uncle Stoppard.

Pablo nodded. "There are a few words I recognize. Some words look similar in both languages. But I can't be certain what it says."

The next day Uncle Stoppard biked over to the University of Minnesota. When he got back at lunchtime, he was sweating and smiling.

"Finn," he said. "You are not going to believe this."

I didn't believe him. Not at first. Uncle Stoppard had gone to the language department at the university and tracked down someone who could read Portuguese. And they translated the entries in Dad's journal. One of the entries was a list that Dad had made of all the Mayan artifacts that he and Mom and the other archeologists had discovered. Uncle Stoppard also had a list. A list of the artifacts that the Ackerberg Institute had taken from our storage room. The black-suited, black-gloved Ackerberg guys had given the list to Uncle Stop as a kind of receipt. Anyway, the two lists were exactly the same. Every artifact that Dad had dug up was recorded in his journal and had eventually been boxed up and flown back to Minneapolis, and then—seven years later—given to the Ackerbergers. Every artifact, except one.

"I don't believe it," I said.

"See, I told you."

"What does this mean?" I pointed to a line in Dad's journal that Uncle Stoppard had circled in red pencil. *Crocodilo de ouro.* "Crocodile?"

"Of gold, Finn! A croc of gold."

"I don't remember seeing a golden crocodile."

"It never reached Minneapolis."

"What happened to it?" I asked. "Was it stolen?"

Dad had written, in one of the journals that I had read, about a mysterious thief at the dig site down in Agualar

"No, not stolen," said Uncle Stoppard. "Buried."

"But it was already buried."

"Your dad reburied it. He writes about it in another entry in Portuguese. *Debaixo de nossa tenda.* He buried the golden crocodile under his tent."

"Why?"

"For safekeeping. Because of the thief. And he listed all the Mayan treasure in Portuguese because he was worried that someone at the campsite, someone he was working with, might turn out to be the thief. Everyone at the camp spoke only English or Spanish, so by keeping an accurate written record in another language, your dad was making sure no one could trick him."

"It's a good thing my parents liked learning other languages," I said. "I mean, *like* learning languages."

"A very good thing," said Uncle Stoppard. "And you'll notice on this list the Ackerberg fellows gave me that there is no mention of a *crocodilo de ouro.*"

I scanned Uncle Stoppard's receipt. "So, if it never reached Minneapolis—?"

"It's still buried under your dad's tent. Or where the

tent used to stand. Remember the hurricane that forced your parents to leave Agualar?"

"Midge."

"Yeah, Midge. In the excitement your dad must have forgotten all about the crocodile."

"Or maybe he didn't have time to un-rebury it."

"It's still down there, Finn! More golden treasure."

"Is it ours?"

"No, it's not ours. But I'll bet the institute would pay big bucks to get their hands on that croc."

Big bucks. Bucks that would pay for Uncle Stoppard and me to fly to Iceland and lead a hunting expedition for my parents. "Where exactly is their institute?"

"No one knows for sure," said Uncle Stoppard. "But they have a website on the Net. And I have their phone number, too."

And now, a month later, Uncle Stoppard and I and our friend Jared were on the road to Agualar. The boiling, burning road. With a poor hitchhiker standing out in the merciless sun.

"See, Uncle Stop," I said. "He's not a mirage."

As our car zoomed closer to the figure, he didn't disappear like those mirages of water on the highway. The figure grew more solid and more colorful. The hitchhiker was a young guy wearing jeans, cowboy boots, and a cowboy hat. A yellowish straw cowboy hat like the one Jared wore. The hitchhiker also wore a bright red, short-sleeved shirt.

"Please, Jared," I said. "Can't we—"

"Sorry, buddy. My job is to keep you boys out of trouble." Jared looked up in the rearview mirror and winked at Uncle Stoppard.

"I thought cops were supposed to help people."

Jared glanced quickly at me. "I am, Finn. I'm making sure you get back to Minneapolis with your head still attached to your shoulders and all your fingers in place."

The hitchhiker stuck his hand out and waved at us. You could practically see the sweat dripping from his forehead beneath the cowboy hat. He smiled. But Jared drove right on by.

"You're mean," I said.

"Thank you," said Jared.

"He didn't look like he was from around here," said Uncle Stoppard.

"Asian," said Jared, glancing into the rearview mirror again.

"Chinese, I think," said Uncle Stoppard.

"Why Chinese?" I asked.

"It's only a guess," said Uncle Stoppard. "But his shirt was like the Chinese flag. Bright red with one big gold star and four smaller ones on the left."

"How do you know so much about flags?" asked Jared.

"I read a lot."

"Why would someone wear a flag?" I asked.

"Well, some American clothes have flag colors on them. You know that one designer guy—what's his name?—and all his clothes are red, white, and blue. Maybe that hitchhiker wants everyone to know where he's from."

What was a Chinese cowboy doing in the middle of the Agualaran desert?

Uncle Stoppard laid down in the backseat. Jared

played one of his Garth Brooks tapes. I still felt sorry for that guy back there on the side of the road. I sat up and turned to look out the back window.

The flat black highway and the flat brown desert were empty.

The Chinese cowboy was gone.

2
The Disappearing Road

"He couldn't disappear," said Uncle Stoppard.

"It's some kind of trick," said Jared.

"But where would he go?" I asked. The desert behind us was empty. No other cars, no rocks, no billboards, no cactus. Nothing to hide behind. If the cowboy was standing, sitting, or lying in the dirt, we would have seen him.

"We've got to go back," I said.

Jared shook his head. "That's just what he wants us to do," he said. "Then he and his buddies will jump out with guns, hijack the car, and leave us stranded in the middle of nowhere."

"Jump out from where?" I asked.

"We are *not* turning round," said Jared. He pushed down on the gas, and we sped even faster toward the Gold Forest.

Where did the cowboy go? It's impossible for someone to disappear like that.

"It's not impossible," said Uncle Stoppard, lying down in the backseat again, "for someone to disappear like that. Maybe he got sucked into another universe."

"Yeah, right," I said.

"Through a cosmic wormhole," he said. "Matter isn't

solid, you know. It's not like a brick. Scientists say it's more like a sponge. Or foam. Full of microscopic bubbles and tunnels and holes. I'm surprised more people don't disappear."

Maybe my parents discovered an Icelandic wormhole.

"I don't care what the scientists say," said Jared. "I say the guy's still back there hiding. He's just waiting for us to turn around and then—bang!"

At least we knew the cowboy was not a mirage. A mirage would have vanished as we drove closer. But maybe the cowboy was something worse. According to my *Manual del Agualar,* people here in Central America believe in spirits and ghosts. They even have a special day to celebrate them, the Day of the Dead. Creepy. A photo in my *Manual* showed a kid eating what looked like a human skull made out of sugar.

The pages in my handbook were flooded with golden light. I looked up and saw that we were completely surrounded by thousands of the giant cacti. Each golden cactus was covered with massive flowers. Orange buds, big as tomatoes, were circled by feathery crowns of yellow petals. A redheaded woodpecker flew over our car.

"Let's stop and take a picture," said Uncle Stoppard.

"Forget it," said Jared. "Look." He pointed to a green metal sign on the right side of the highway that displayed words in Spanish and English: NO STOPPING FOR ANY REASON.

The Golden Finger cacti reminded me of monster yellow gloves jammed into the ground. How did the highway workers make this road without getting needled to death? They must have worn suits of armor.

"With this many cacti, there's got to be water nearby," said Jared.

"Or underground streams," said Uncle Stoppard.

The cactus fields sloped downward. Soon the cacti were replaced by tall grassy bushes.

Agualar is a long, skinny country, shaped like a strip of bacon, that stretches along the Gulf of Mexico. Inside Agualar itself, the country is divided into three separate strips. First, there's the desert strip that connects with Mexico on the west. Next comes the jungly-foresty-riverish strip in the middle, where the campsite is. And then the sandy coastal strip on the east. The tall grassy bushes marked the border where the desert strip meets the jungle region.

We saw another sign: CHUCA. 5 KM.

It was a hundred degrees outside, but I felt goose bumps run up and down my arms. Chuca was the name of the village near my parent's dig site. Where I had played in the Agualaran sun as a little kid. I don't have any memories of feeling really hot. Not hot like I felt now. Maybe, as you grow older and your skin stretches, there's more of you to get warm. More surface area.

A moment later we drove onto a rickety wooden bridge.

"Jared!" yelled Uncle Stoppard. "Didn't you read that sign?"

"Yeah, it said Chuca, five kilometers."

"No, the other one. Next to the bridge. It said: PROCEED AT YOUR OWN RISK. BRIDGE WEAKENED BY HURRICANE.

"Oops."

Thirty feet below, a stream ran through a narrow, rocky gorge. The Pellagro River that Dad had described in his journals. It looked peaceful, and the water was as brown as root beer. I knew that just below the surface, according to my dad's journal, crocodiles pursued small fish for dinner. Downriver, near my parents' former campsite, the river grew wider and faster. It was hard to believe that in a few miles the gentle river below us ended in a dangerous waterfall. A waterfall where the canoe carrying my aunt Verona, who had worked with Mom and Dad at the campsite, had met its deadly end seven years ago.

When our car reached the other side of the bridge—safely—Jared yelled, "Yee-hah! Don't believe everything you read."

"I believe this map," said Uncle Stoppard. "And it says that a dirt road will be coming up on your left."

"Yeah, I see it," Jared said.

"Turn here. This road should lead us all the way to the campsite."

The winding dirt road slanted sharply down between walls of tall waving grass. The grass blades, as thick and flat as water skis, were golden-brown at the bottom, bright green at the tips. The tips swayed several feet above the roof of our car.

"Um, Stoppard. We have a problem." Jared stopped the car.

The dirt road lasted only about a hundred feet. We were staring at the side of a small hill.

"Something's wrong," said Uncle Stoppard.

"Yeah," said Jared. "The road disappears."

"Just like the Chinese cowboy," I said.

Jared turned off the Garth Brooks tape. Unseen insects buzzed around us in the grass.

"I don't like sitting here," said Jared. "It makes me nervous." He took off his yellow cowboy hat and threw it in the backseat. "We're backing up," he said.

"It's Midge," said Uncle Stoppard.

Jared stomped on the brake. "Where?"

"No, I mean the hurricane," said Uncle Stoppard. "I'll bet that's why this hill is here. Remember those hurricanes that struck Honduras? All the huge mudslides they caused? This hill was probably part of the slopes we just drove down."

The hill was as tall as our apartment building back home and was covered with bristly, brownish grass. A giant sleeping porcupine.

"Do you think the camp is covered in mud, too?" I asked.

"I didn't think of that," said Uncle Stoppard.

Was the Golden Crocodile of the Mayas buried under a ton of hard, grassy mud? If my parents and I had stayed behind, and not fled from the hurricane, our tent would have been crushed beneath a sliding hillside, a glacier of dirt. Would we have been buried alive?

"What happened to everyone who worked with my parents?" I asked Uncle Stoppard.

"What do you mean?"

"When the hurricane came, did everyone leave?"

"They had to."

"Yeah, but did everyone escape?"

"I suppose so," he said. "Why do you—? Oh." Uncle Stoppard thought of it now, too.

"Oh," said Jared. He thought the same thing. Human skeletons waiting to be uncovered along with the Mayan gold. Crocodiles and archeologists buried side by side.

"So how do we find the rest of the road?" Jared asked. He looked around nervously. The tall grass blocked our vision on both sides.

"Maybe the road is on the other side of the hill," I said.

"We're not getting out of the car to find out," said Jared.

"What's that!" I yelled.

Everyone jumped.

Someone had touched my neck. No, it was sweat running down from my head. I hadn't noticed how hot I was since Jared had stopped the car.

"That buzzing is driving me nuts," said Jared. "Let's get out of here."

"Do you hear that?" asked Uncle Stoppard.

"I don't hear anything except those blasted insects."

I heard it. A man's voice. Very far away. And the American word "Help."

"There it is again," said Uncle Stoppard. The water-ski grass rustled softly.

"You guys are giving me the creeps," Jared said.

"Let's drive into Chuca," said Uncle Stop. "We could use the break. And I need to stretch. We can ask someone in town if another road leads down toward the river."

But Jared couldn't back the car up any farther. Another car had appeared out of nowhere, blocking our path. Men carrying pistols and rifles jumped out of the car and surrounded us.

3
Santa Mona

"Drug dealers," said Jared.

The four men surrounding our rental car wore sandy-brown uniforms, black boots, mirror sunglasses, and shiny gold badges on their chests.

"They're not drug dealers," said Uncle Stoppard. "They're the police."

"I mean," said Jared, "they think *we* are drug dealers."

"Step out of the car," bawled one of the Agualaran cops. He was bald and wore a thick black mustache. He aimed a thick black gun straight at Jared's head.

"It's all right," said Jared.

The three of us opened the car doors and stepped out. Heat rose up from the dusty road. The metal side of the car felt as hot as our apartment radiators in winter.

"This is all a mistake," said Uncle Stoppard. "We are—"

"American?" asked the bald cop. He must have been their leader.

We all three nodded.

"Why are you on this road?" asked the cop.

"We were going to a campsite by the river," said Uncle Stoppard.

"This road does not go to the river."

"We figured that out," said Jared.

"So, why are you on this road?" repeated the cop.

"Our map said this was the right road," said Uncle Stoppard.

"Where are you from?"

"North," I said. The cops all stared at me. "Um, *el norte?*"

"Look here," said Jared. He reached into the back pocket of his jeans for his wallet. All four cops clicked their guns. All four barrels were aimed at Jared's sweaty forehead. At that moment I wished Jared and Uncle Stoppard and I could have been sucked into another universe.

"Careful guys," Jared said. "I'm just getting my ID. You know, *identificación.*"

"I know what it means," said the head cop.

Jared flipped his wallet open and held it up for the cop to read. The cop scratched his thick black mustache and stared at Jared. "American police?"

Jared nodded. "And the three of us are here on vacation."

"We got lost," said Uncle Stoppard.

"You have a gun?" asked the cop.

Jared nodded again. "Packed in my suitcase."

Uncle Stoppard stared at me. He didn't know that Jared had brought a gun, either. It's a good thing I liked Mexican food. They probably serve you tacos in prison down here.

"We need to search your car," said the bald cop.

"Be my guest," said Jared.

The bald guy and a partner opened our car and

pulled all our luggage onto the dirt road. While the other two cops kept their guns aimed at us, their buddies unlocked each suitcase, un-Velcroed each travel bag, and unzipped each backpack. I felt we stood on that hot dirt road for hours. They even searched inside our socks and shoes. Not the ones we were wearing. We had to show them our passports, and the tourist cards we each got back at the airport. The cards told them how long we were staying in Agualar.

"One week?" asked one of the cops.

"It's a vacation," lied Uncle Stoppard.

Uncle Stoppard also had to show them proof that I wasn't being kidnapped. Every year kids are kidnapped from the United States and Canada and brought down to Mexico. They're usually kidnapped by one parent who's divorcing the other one. And since the cops saw two guys with a teenager, they wanted to make sure that Uncle Stoppard and Jared weren't criminals. Clever Uncle Stop had asked a lawyer friend of his back in Minneapolis to make out a paper proving that he was my legal guardian. Until my folks get back from Iceland.

"What's this?" said the bald cop. He held up a paperback book he found among Uncle Stoppard's underwear. Red letters, dripping in gore, spelled out the title: *Shoot, Stab, and Strangle.* It was one of Uncle Stop's reference books that he uses while working on a new mystery. This particular book describes all the different ways people are murdered. The bald guy was flipping through the pages, probably looking at photos of people who were shot, stabbed, or suffocated to death.

"That's mine," said Uncle Stoppard.

Great! The police knew that Jared had a gun and that Uncle Stoppard was reading about killing people.

"He doesn't really murder people," I said.

"Finn—!"

"He just writes about it."

"A reporter?" asked the bald guy.

One of the other cops mumbled, "Television."

Uncle Stoppard shook his head. "No, I'm a writer. An author."

"Autor," translated Jared.

The cops didn't look convinced. A big wrestler-type guy with arm muscles bulging out of his short-sleeved police shirt grunted something. He pulled a small object out of my backpack and handed it to his boss. The bald guy shook the object in front of Uncle Stoppard's face. "Is this yours, *señor?"* he asked.

"Uh, well—"

"That belongs to me," I said. It was a paperback mystery with a dead body on the cover, a dead body sprawled over a giant tube of toothpaste. The mystery was not one that Uncle Stoppard had written. The bald cop stared at the cover, flipped the book over, and then smiled.

"Ahhh," he said. "Mona Trafalgar-Squeer."

"Ahhh," echoed the other cops.

Mona Trafalgar-Squeer is probably the most stunning mystery writer in the world. Next to Uncle Stoppard, I mean. Critics call her the Princess of Puzzles, the Baroness of Bafflement, the Queen of Crime. Uncle Stoppard says it's a crime her books even sell. Mona was born in England and is still a British citizen, but she spends her summers in Minneapolis, where she zips around on a giant silver motorcycle or else spends months locked in her apartment overlooking the Mississippi River. She's published a lot of mysteries. Just like Uncle Stoppard. I don't know why, but for some reason she and Uncle Stop aren't exactly pals.

Mona's plots are the best. They are galactic. You can never figure out her puzzles until the last page. It's no surprise to me that she's one of the best-selling authors in the world. Her books are translated into fourteen different languages including, we found out, Spanish.

The cop read out the title of Mona's book for the benefit of his buddies. *"Shrunken Eds."*

"Oooh," said the other cops.

Shrunken Eds is Mona's newest mystery. All of the victims are named Ed (Edgar, Edison, Edwina, etc.). The villain, the evil Duchess of DeMonica, has developed a diabolical chemical which shrinks human beings down to three inches. She slips the chemical into each Ed by various means, in their food or toothpaste, waits for them to shrink, and then uses a high-tech vacuum cleaner to suction them through keyholes or under doors. No one can figure out how the victim's bodies keep disappearing from securely locked rooms.

Uncle Stoppard said he thought Mona's plot sucked.

"You can borrow it," I told the cop. I had already finished reading it during the nine-hour drive from Mexico City.

The bald cop looked at Uncle Stoppard. "You are a writer, too."

"Uh, yes," said Uncle Stoppard.

"From Minneapolis," I said. "That's where Mona lives, too, you know."

The bald cop asked, "Have you ever seen Señorita Mona?"

"Seen her? She and my uncle are practically best friends!"

All the cops immediately asked for Uncle Stoppard's autograph. Luckily, Uncle Stoppard also had a few copies of his own books (he always travels with them) with his picture on the back covers. It's the picture I snapped in our sunroom back home.

"Sorry, *señor.* We thought you were drug dealers," said the big cop with the muscular arms. "Not writer friends of *la grande Mona.*"

They let us go, but they kept Jared's gun. Even though he worked with law enforcement, it was still illegal to bring any kind of gun into Mexico or Agualar from another country. Jared's gun (a Smith and Wesson .357 Magnum, Model 65, made of stainless steel) would be kept at police headquarters in the nearby town of Juanpablo (a brand-new town, named for the Pope, and built after Hurricane Midge). Jared would be able to pick it up as soon as our "vacation" was over and we were headed back to *el norte.*

The cops told us that the old river road continued on the other side of Chuca. They gave Jared directions, asked Uncle Stoppard to greet Mona for them the next time he saw her, and drove off in their car. By this time the sun was beginning to set. The tall grasses were growing full of shadows. We had to repack all our luggage and haul it back into the car.

"Those guys sure made a mess," I said. "They should have helped us clean it up."

Uncle Stoppard was smashing stuff into his suitcase. *"La grande Mona,"* he mumbled.

"Thanks for keeping our butts out of prison, pal," Jared said to me. "It's a good thing you're a celebrity, Stoppard. I mean, good thing you *know* a celebrity."

Uncle Stoppard shot a glance at Jared and then crawled into the backseat of the car. "I need another can of pop," he said.

The town of Chuca was ten buildings and a dog. Five buildings on the left of the highway, five buildings on the right, and the dog stood in the middle and barked at us. Actually, it wasn't a highway anymore, but a dirt road. A blind person could tell when he reached Chuca. The car dropped about six inches as the asphalt stopped and the dirt began. I bounced up and hit the ceiling. Uncle Stoppard's pop can flew out of his hand and fizzed all over his khaki pants. The three of us laughed.

"I guess we can say we dropped into town," said Uncle Stoppard.

Chuca was quiet. No one on the street. The barking dog had run away. A red-and-white Coke sign glowed in a window. Somewhere a radio was playing rock music. But not a single Chucan in sight. In the distance, off to our right, we saw some cars and bright lights in a field. It looked like a big parking lot.

"Here's our turn," said Jared.

A bumpy road veered to the left. The car's bouncing headlights illuminated dark scraggy trees, giant palms, bushy clumps of wild sugarcane. We were surrounded again by the buzz of invisible insects.

Nothing looked familiar to me. Of course, I was just a kid when I was in Agualar the last time, but shouldn't some memory come popping into my brain?

What would the old campsite look like? Would the grassy ground still be pitted with old holes made by the archeologists? Would we recognize any landmarks from the photos that Dad and Mom had taken seven years ago? Or maybe we would find another giant sleeping porcupine. A huge new hill of mud and grass. How would we know when to stop the car?

Jared knew when to stop the car.

We all knew.

Goose bumps ran up and down my arms again. Somehow, the three of us had traveled backward in time. Backward seven years. Ahead of us lay the old campsite in a small, natural clearing, complete with tents, lanterns, Jeeps, and moving, breathing human beings.

4
The Dinosaur Hunters

A tall, elderly woman in dark work pants, blue shirt-sleeves rolled up to her elbows, and short silver hair walked over to our car. "I'm Dr. Himmelfarben," she said. "May I help you?"

Behind her stood a short, round man with white hair that defied gravity and sprang out in a dozen directions. Einstein hair.

"And this," said the woman, "is—"

"I'm sure these people know who I am, Doctor," said the little man. "I'm Professor Freaze. Professor Tuscan Freaze?"

He said his name like a question. Since the three of us didn't know what the answer was, we all kept quiet.

"You're not from the institute, are you?" said the professor.

"Institute?" Jared said.

"I'm Stoppard Sterling. The writer. From Minnesota. And this is my nephew, Finn. And this is—"

The professor turned abruptly. "I don't have time for this," he said over his shoulder to the doctor. "You deal with these people." He marched away toward one of the tents.

Dr. Himmelfarben waved her hands. She looked embarrassed. "It's been a very busy time for us," she said. "We weren't expecting anyone. We thought you might be from the institute."

"Which institute is that?" asked Uncle Stoppard.

"The Ackerberg Institute, of course. You've heard of it?"

The three of us looked at one another.

"From your reactions," said the doctor, "I'd say that you have indeed heard of it."

"We're looking for a campsite," I said.

"It looks as though you've found one," said the doctor.

"I mean, an old campsite. Where there used to be an archeological dig."

"This is it," said the doctor.

"The old Zwake site?" said Uncle Stoppard.

"You're familiar with their work?"

"He's familiar with me," I said. "The old Zwakes were my parents."

Dr. Himmelfarben looked at me carefully.

"I'm the new Zwake," I said.

"Where are my manners?" said the doctor. "Come. Join us. We were just having coffee with our dessert." When the doctor smiled, I was reminded of a Tyrannosaurus Rex. Neat little rows of sharp white teeth.

The doctor introduced us to a group of four people sitting around a small campfire. As the doctor hunted up three more chairs for us to sit on, another guy with frizzy Einstein hair, dark hair this time, shook our hands. "Hello, I'm Professor Freaze's son—Dr. Tulsa Freaze," he said. "And this is my wife, Fleur."

Fleur was pretty. Long blond hair, pretty green eyes, but too skinny.

"Would you like some coffee?" she said.

"Um, do you have any beer?" asked Jared.

The guy sitting next to Tulsa reached into a metal cooler beside his chair and handed two icy bottles to Jared and Uncle Stoppard. "You from the States?" he said. He tossed me a frosty can of pop. He had thick, wavy black hair, dark brown eyes, and a goatee. A gold earring gleamed in each ear, and a gold cross glittered on a thin chain round his neck.

"From Minnesota," Jared said.

"Ah, snow country," said Tulsa.

The guy with the goatee and the cross leaned over from his chair and shook hands with Jared and Uncle Stoppard. "José Mirón," he said. "Call me Zé."

Dr. Himmelfarben nodded toward a third man, sitting on a stool. "And this is Gabriel Paz," she said. "Our colleague from Ecuador." Gabriel Paz was quiet. He politely sipped at his coffee while staring at us through thick glasses. Everyone else wore work shirts and pants or shorts, but Paz wore khakis like Uncle Stoppard (without the pop stains), a crisp white shirt, and a royal blue tie. He reminded me more of a high school principal than of a scientist who liked to mess around in the dirt.

"Are you guys archeologists, too?" I asked.

Dr. Himmelfarben waved at me. "This young gentleman is the son of the famous Zwake team."

Tulsa leaned forward in his camp chair. "Ah, the ones who disappeared in Greenland?"

"It was Iceland," said Dr. Himmelfarben. "Correct?"

"Yeah," I said.

"That was a long time ago," said Zé.

"Seven years," I said.

"Finn was with his parents at the time," said Uncle Stoppard. "Here in Agualar."

Gabriel Paz nodded gravely and sipped his coffee.

"Does it look familiar?" said Fleur. "The campsite, I mean."

"It's hard to tell in the dark," I said.

"We'll take you on a tour tomorrow morning," said Dr. Himmelfarben.

"Oh, and the trailer," said Fleur, smiling at the doctor.

The doctor flashed her dinosaur teeth. "Yes. The trailer. We have a surprise for you gentlemen."

Surprise?

"To answer your question, young man," said Tulsa Freaze. "We're not archeologists. We are dinosaur hunters."

From the way Frizzy Freaze said the word *archeologists*, he obviously thought his reason for digging holes was more important than my parents' reason.

"You look for bones?" I said.

"And plants," said Fleur. "That's Dr. Himmelfarben's and Mr. Paz's specialty."

"Really? That reminds me," Jared said. "I've got a question about those Golden Fingers we drove through this afternoon."

"Paleobotany," said Dr. Himmelfarben, "is the study of *extinct* plant life. Which can tell us a great deal about early conditions on our planet. Climate, insect life, the digestive system of dinosaurs."

"How long have you been down here?" asked Uncle Stoppard.

"Four months," said Tulsa Freaze.

"Why here?" I asked. "I mean, in this spot."

Tulsa jerked a thumb behind him, toward the tents. "Walk five miles thataway, straight east of here, and you'll run into the Gulf of Mexico. And four hundred miles out into the Gulf of Mexico lies an underwater crater."

"Chicxulub," said Gabriel Paz.

"Gesundheit," said Uncle Stoppard.

"That," said Gabriel Paz slowly, "is the name of the crater. Chik shoo loob."

"I better go see if your father wants some more coffee," said Fleur. She grabbed an extra mug and wandered toward the tents. I could tell by the look on Tulsa Freaze's face that he did not like being interrupted.

"Chicxulub," he continued in a louder voice, "is the largest meteor crater found on the planet. One hundred and twenty-five miles in diameter. Big enough to hold New York City, Philadelphia, and Washington, D.C., all at the same time. The meteor that created Chicxulub is also responsible for killing all the earth's dinosaurs."

My fifth-grade science teacher back in Minneapolis, Mr. Thomas, once gave me a stunning book about the destruction of the dinosaurs. It explains how scientists believe that 60 million years ago, a gigantic comet or meteor collided with the Earth, spraying tons and tons of dirt into the atmosphere. The dirt and dust darkened the sky and choked off the sunlight for years. Temperatures dropped. Plants wilted and died. Plant-eating dinosaurs, like stegosaurs and triceratops, along with dinosaur-eating dinosaurs, like the T. Rex, all eventually starved to death. Glaciers covered the continents. Then the dirt slowly filtered back down to the ground, the sky cleared up, and the sunlight returned to Earth. At least that's the theory.

According to Tulsa Freaze, the meteor broke off from a larger asteroid called the Death Star.

"Its full name is the 26-Million-Year Death Star," said Tulsa. "Because it swings by the Earth every 26 million years."

"You mean, it's coming back?"

"Don't worry, Finn," said Uncle Stoppard. "We'll be home by then."

"If the meteor hit four hundred miles away," said Jared, "why are you guys here in Agualar?"

"Floods," said Zé.

"Which I was going to explain," said Tulsa.

Zé ignored him. It was his turn to talk. "When the meteor hit, the impact sent a wall of water racing outward in all directions. The dinosaurs that lived closest to the impact were killed immediately. Drowned."

"Or buried," said Tulsa.

"Buried under tons of mud," said Zé. "Mud that formed from the water and dust shot up by the meteor."

"Which means," said Gabriel Paz, "that the dinosaurs buried in Agualar and Central America should be better preserved than the dinosaurs that died out gradually in other areas of the world."

"Dinosaurs that died in the open air were vulnerable to predators," said Tulsa.

"And to the weather," said Gabriel Paz.

"And to natural disasters like fires," said Zé. "Dinosaurs buried under the mud are, we hope, more intact."

"Have you found any?" I asked.

"Better than that," said Tulsa. "We found—"

"Eggs!" said all three dinosaur hunters in unison.

Zé shifted in his chair. The firelight gleamed off the cross on his chest. "We think this area may have been a nesting ground," he said.

"For which dinosaurs?" said Uncle Stoppard.

"A newly discovered dinosaur," said Gabriel Paz. "The Paziosaurus."

"The Tuscanosaurus," said Tulsa.

The two men glared at each other.

"We really haven't given it a name," said Zé. "Yet."

"It has a name," said Gabriel.

"Damn right it has," said Tulsa.

"About sixty million years ago," said Zé, "the land-masses which eventually became known as Central and South America were not attached to each other. Not yet. Water flowed between them, a shallow sea full of weeds and algae, connecting the Atlantic and the Pacific oceans. Well, according to samples we've recently uncovered, we think we've discovered a new breed of dinosaur that lived partially on land and partially in the water. And we also think the creatures—"

"The Tuscanosaurs," said Tulsa.

"—swam across the shallow sea between prehistoric Agualar and prehistoric Ecuador."

"Isn't that a long way?" I said.

"Whales swim farther than that on a regular basis," said Paz.

"The Tuscanosaurs liked to lay their eggs in burrows or underground tunnels," said Tulsa.

"And Agualar is full of tunnels," Zé said. "This whole country is one gigantic shelf of limestone jutting out into the gulf, and limestone is the perfect material for forming tunnels and caves."

Like the microscopic sponge-foam Uncle Stoppard talked about. Wormholes.

"We think," Zé said, "that the dinosaurs may have swum here each year in order to lay their eggs."

"So there could be Pazio—uh, Tuscano—um, dinosaur eggs right under our feet?" I said.

"Or closer," said Gabriel Paz.

The campfire crackled and hissed.

"You said you already found some eggs," Uncle Stoppard said.

"We can show you in the morning," said Tulsa. He stood up and emptied the rest of his coffee into the fire. "Actually, we were just discussing hitting the sack when we saw your headlights. Morning comes pretty early round here." Zé and Gabriel Paz remained seated.

"Nobody's going into town?" asked Jared.

"Nothing to see," said Zé.

"Except for the magic show," said Gabriel Paz.

"Magic?" I said.

"A traveling carnival," said Zé. "Over by Chuca." That explained the cars and lights we saw in the big field just outside of town. "It's supposed to be a family of magicians from Mexico," he said.

"If you care for that sort of thing," said Tulsa.

"What do you say, Finn? Shall we go over now?"

"Now? We need to set up our tent, Uncle Stoppard. And get something to eat."

And make our plans for finding the golden crocodile.

"You're welcome to the rest of our dessert," said Zé. "If you like apple strudel. Dr. Himmelfarben made it."

Where was Dr. Himmelfarben? She had disappeared during the talk about the Death Star. Probably asleep in her tent. Fleur hadn't come back, either. Or the rude Professor Freaze. Frizzy Senior.

Uncle Stoppard and Jared and I set up our tent next to our car. It was one of those six-sided models supported by long metal tubes which crisscross over each other and form a big beehive shape. The tent can hold up to six people, so we had plenty of room for all our luggage. After a quick meal of grilled cheese sandwiches, baked beans, lukewarm pop, and apple strudel, we slid into our sleeping bags and Uncle Stoppard switched off the electric lantern.

Inside, our cozy hexagon was inky black. Outside, the night was abuzz with insects. An occasional bark from that dog back in Chuca. I could hear the soothing murmur of the nearby river. Soothing. Flowing. Streaming.

"Uncle Stoppard?"

"Yes, Finn?"

"I need to, um, get rid of some pop."

"All right, but stay close to the tent."

"Not too close," added Jared.

I unzipped the entrance to the tent and stepped outside. Pale silver starlight filtered through the trees touching every tent, every tree, every blade of grass. The red flames of the dying campfire dimly reflected off the beer cooler. Enough light for me to carefully pick my way toward a tree a few yards behind our tent.

Ouch! A sharp pain zigzagged through my right foot. As I reached down and rubbed the sole, my fingers found a large sliver protruding from the skin. I yanked it free and held it up to my glasses. The sliver was thick and hairy. It looked like a sticker from a plant. A cactus needle?

That sound again! A man's voice crying for help. The same voice Uncle Stoppard and I had heard right before the cops almost arrested us.

The voice came from the direction of the river. Clear, but faint. Ghosts? The spirits of angry Maya whose treasure had been disturbed by members of my family years ago? Perhaps the notorious Curse of the Zwakes had returned.

I decided I'd take only a few more steps, and then return to the tent. The ground disappeared from beneath my feet. My butt and sneakers struck a steep, sloping wall of dirt. I rolled over and over about twenty times until my face finally landed in a mound of soft, earthy darkness. Yuck! I spat out a mouthful of damp Agualaran dirt.

Was this one of the holes left over from the archeological dig? I fell into a pit dug by my own parents! Maybe this was the same pit that once held the golden crococdile. Maybe it was a newer hole gouged out by the force of Hurricane Midge or the shovels of the dinosaur hunters.

The star-filled sky took shape overhead. I could make out the blacker, rough edges of the rectangular pit into which I had fallen. The murmur of the invisible river was no longer soothing. It sounded like the chanting of vengeful Mayan ghosts.

In one corner of the pit the chanting grew louder.

Against the dark wall of earth crouched a darker shape. The shape moved, wriggling like a serpent, or a Paziosaur, or a Tuscanosaur. The shadow sprouted arms and floated toward me.

5
The Worm Tunnel

Stuck inside my suitcase, jammed into a smaller blue canvas travel bag, lies a knife. The handle is buffalo bone and the blade is iron. Modern knives have steel blades, but this knife was made before the Civil War by a Blackfoot warrior. The knife was handed down from father to son, until one summer, at an archeological dig in Montana ten years ago, a Blackfoot chieftain gave the knife to my dad as a gift for saving the chief's son from a landslide. My dad's lucky hunting knife. It had saved my life once before. As the snaky shadow in the pit drew nearer, I wished the knife were in my hand instead of back in my suitcase.

The shadow moaned. "Ohhhhhhhhh."

The screams woke up the campsite. My screams. The shadow froze. I heard Uncle Stoppard's and Jared's voices yelling from a distance.

"Hurry! Hurry, down here!" I cried.

Flashlight beams pierced the darkness, flooding the pit.

From overhead came Tulsa's voice, "Who is that?"

"It's the Zwake boy," said Dr. Himmelfarben.

"No, I mean *him*."

The former shadow wore a bright red, short-sleeve shirt decorated with five gold stars. It was the Chinese cowboy, boots and all. His yellow straw hat was missing. He looked about Jared's age. Tall, with scared eyes, hair thick with mud, and cuts and scrapes crisscrossing his bare arms. A purple bruise glowed under his left eye.

"I think my foot is broke," said the cowboy. His stumbling movements, his arms groping for balance, looked less snakey in the brilliance of six or seven flashlights.

The cowboy and I were hauled out of the pit by a multitude of arms. He lay down on the wet dewy grass, breathing heavily. Dr. Himmelfarben knelt next to his feet, feeling for broken bones.

"Finn! What were you doing?" asked Uncle Stoppard.

"Getting rid of some pop, remember?"

"Way over here?"

"I heard someone. That voice we heard by the tall grass, remember?"

Later that morning, at breakfast (Dr. Himmelfarben invited us over for potato pancakes, sausages, and oatmeal), we learned that it was the Chinese cowboy we had heard when we stopped the car. He had been calling for help. From underground.

Nixon Wu was from China. He was a paleontologist, along with his father, Ching-chi Wu, and had worked at digs all over China and Mongolia. The Wus had been among the scientists who dug up the dinosaur eggs in Mongolia, the largest collection of prehistoric eggs ever discovered. When Nixon had heard from fellow scientists in America that the famous Professor Tuscan Freaze was hunting for eggs in Agualar, he decided to

visit him and offer his services. But on the drive from
Mexico City, Nixon had stopped to pick up a hitchhiker
in the Agualaran desert. The hitchhiker pulled a gun on
poor Nixon, stole his wallet, threw him out of the car
(that held all his luggage), and left him stranded by the
side of the road. At this point in Nixon's story, Jared
gave me a knowing look while he shoveled eggs into his
mouth. Chicken eggs, not dinosaur.

Nixon decided, after his car had been hijacked, to
continue on to Agualar. Where else could he go? Hours
trudged by before he saw another car on the road. Our
car. The car with the mean driver. And while Nixon
watched us drive by, he felt the ground give way beneath his feet. He slipped into a hole.

"A wormhole," said Uncle Stoppard.

"A sinkhole," said Zé. "A well in the limestone. There
are hundreds of these natural wells all over the Yucatan.
They call them *cenotes.*"

The bottom of Nixon's *cenote* slanted downward.
Once he sank below the surface of the desert, his feet
slipped. He was caught in a fast-flowing stream of water,
shooting through a smooth, limestone tunnel. A giant
water slide. One tunnel fed into another, dropping him
down to lower and lower levels.

Finally Nixon's downward ride stopped. He said there
was enough light to make out a huge cavern filled with
a pool. He swam to the side of the pool and pulled himself up to a rocky ledge. He then heard the sound of
rushing water. He thought it was a way out. He followed
the sound and then slipped into another tunnel. The
powerful current held him underwater. In a few mo-
ments his head broke the surface. He found himself in a

river. The Pellagro. Afraid that he might encounter an Agualaran crocodile, he quickly crawled up the bank and lay down. It was evening by this time. He saw the lights from the campsite. He was bruised, bloody, and exhausted, but he could still walk. As he neared the camp, Nixon fell into the pit where I found him. He passed out. My stumbling into the pit woke him up. He said he thought I was a ghost.

"People believe in ghosts down here," I whispered to Uncle Stoppard.

The dinosaur hunters were very excited by Nixon's story. They kept asking all kinds of questions about the tunnels. Especially about the cavern and the pool.

Dr. Himmelfarben said that Nixon was lucky. He had only sprained his ankle, she said, and should stay off his feet for a few days.

"But, Doctor," said Tulsa. "We need Wu to take us back to the cavern."

"I think it can wait," said the doctor.

"Not if our theory is correct," said Zé.

The Paziosaur or Tuscanosaur eggs found in Agualar had all been located near the mouths of narrow tunnels. And all the eggs had been broken.

"Dinosaur eggs go bad?" I asked.

"Isn't that exciting?" said Fleur. "Moldy eggs are full of prehistoric plant life."

"And bug life," said Dr. Himmelfarben. "If a dinosaur egg broke, ancient beetles may have crawled inside the shell and laid their eggs. The yolks provided nourishment for the larvae. If we're lucky," she said, turning to me, "an egg might contain fossilized frass."

"Frass?" I said.

"Insect droppings," said Gabriel Paz.

"Pupa poop," said Zé.

Uncle Stoppard gazed down at his oatmeal. He handed the plate over to me. "Finn, you want to finish this?"

Nixon's story excited the dinosaur hunters because they believed all the single eggs found so far had actually come from a central location. Eggs were normally laid in groups. And usually in a nest or protective pit. Since the newly discovered dinosaur (the Paz or the Tusk) was supposedly a burrower and a swimmer, the scientists figured that the central location for the eggs was probably underground and near water. Like Nixon's cavern.

We were almost finished with breakfast when Professor Freaze, Frizzy Senior, joined us. One thing about Einstein hair, it always looks the same, day or night. *Disheveled* is the word Uncle Stoppard used. While the Professor scooped pancakes onto his plate, the other dinosaur hunters filled him in on Nixon's adventures through the limestone labyrinth.

Professor Freaze rolled his eyes. "What have I been telling you for the past four months?" he said. "I feel like I'm back teaching a classroom of freshmen. Of course there's an underground cavern. Why else do you think we're in this hellhole?"

I thought Zé had called it a sinkhole.

"Why else," continued the Professor, "do we have that blasted Arm with us?"

Arm? I looked at Uncle Stoppard. He seemed puzzled, too.

The Professor grabbed a can of mineral water from the cooler. "You all behave as if this were news."

"It *is* news," said Gabriel Paz.

"Good news," added Fleur.

"Maybe to you," said the Professor. "Anyone who has been listening to me realizes that finding the cavern was simply a matter of time."

"Retracing Nixon's cavern will help speed things along, Dad," said Tulsa.

"Patience," said Professor Freaze. "Patience is more important than speed. The dinosaur eggs have been here for millions of years. I'm sure they'll wait for us." He chuckled. "And I hardly think it's Mr. Nixon's cavern. Where did you say you were from, young man?"

"Beijing."

"I remember Beijing. Or Peking. Or whatever they're calling it now. Rude people, boring food, and dangerously inefficient technology." He speared a sausage on the end of his fork. "I'm surprised they even grasp the concept of electricity over there."

"We have Coca-Cola," said Nixon, not smiling.

"Welcome to the New World," said the professor. "And please feel free to observe us at your leisure."

Nixon straighted up in his chair."I thought perhaps," he said, "that you might be able to use another experienced egg-hound, sir."

"Egg-hound?" The professor rolled his eyes, then turned to Dr. Himmelfarben. "I'll be warming up the Arm." He walked away from the campfire, balancing his mineral water on his plate.

Zé swore. Fleur's face turned bright red.

"I'll get you some more painkillers, Mr. Wu," said Dr. Himmelfarben.

Why would anyone travel thousands of miles to work with Professor Freeze?

Breakfast over, Uncle Stoppard and Jared and I walked back to our tent.

"What about the trailer?" I asked.

"Trailer?" said Uncle Stoppard.

"Last night, they said they had a surprise for us in the trailer."

"I think we better let them work. We need to plan our own excavations."

By reading Dad's journals and looking at the photos taken of the old campsite, we were able to reconstruct where everything used to stand. While Jared and Uncle Stoppard looked at the photos, I went out and studied the campsite. I drew a map, marking trees, tents, pits, the trailer, the portable john, the river.

And I met the Arm. It was a motorized vehicle the size of a Jeep with a long, mechanized arm built onto the back. Fleur called it a "cherry picker." The arm could extend about twenty feet and came with a load of attachments, like a vacuum cleaner. The end of the Arm could be fitted with a shovel, a drill, a claw with two-foot-long fingers, a hook, a metal loop that expanded or constricted like a noose, and a razor-edged, deadly looking blade. And it hardly made any noise at all. As I watched Professor Freeze steer it toward the river, bouncing slightly on its fat, balloony tires, all I heard was a faint, low hum.

"The institute spares no expense," Zé said. "The newest equipment, the smartest computers. Now, if they could only send food."

The tents were an original Ackerberg product. They

looked like the old-fashioned kind of cabin-shaped tents, all five staked out in a semicircle around the campfire, but the fabric was lightweight ("The same stuff astronauts wear," said Zé), black (the Ackerberg favorite color), and rip-proof. Zippers all had inside and outside locks, an extra layer of mosquito-proof webbing hung inside the tents, and electric outlets were sewn into the fabric so the campers could connect up to an outside outlet without letting the bugs inside. Each tent had a front entrance flap and windows on three sides made from the bug-proof webbing. If the campers wanted privacy, they zipped down an inside flap and snapped it into place.

Walking back to Uncle Stoppard's hexagon, I saw Fleur outside her tent, stuffing things into a knapsack. I asked her about the surprise she and Dr. Himmelfarben had mentioned last night.

"I'm sorry," she said. "It's been another one of those days. And we're expecting the Ackerberg Institute people to show up anytime now. We'll look at it tomorrow, I promise."

Uncle Stoppard and Jared had finished piecing together the clues about my parents' old campsite. They were sitting in the shade, on a couple of lawn chairs, drinking pop. Spread out on the short, dry grass in front of them were Dad's journals, notebooks, and dozens of old color photos. The two had drawn their own map.

"These photos helped a lot," said Uncle Stoppard.

"See that big tree over there?" Jared pointed. "That weird crooked branch? It's here in this picture, too."

"Good thing Midge didn't blow it over," I said.

I handed over my map.

"Good work," said Uncle Stoppard. "Now all we have to do is compare these two plans and—"

Jared groaned.

I could now see why this campsite had been chosen by two separate groups of scientists, the Zwake team and the Freaze team. The site was near freshwater, on high enough ground to avoid flooding from normal rainfall, within a convenient, natural clearing, and close enough to Chucan civilization for emergency supplies or an occasional cheeseburger. But who could have imagined how similiar both camps would turn out to be? Uncle Stoppard had penned a fat, red X on his map, marking the former site of my parents' tent, pinpointing the exact location of the golden croc.

On my map the exact same spot was currently occupied by another reptile: Professor Tuscan Freaze.

6
Dealing with Reptiles

One of the sections in my *Manual del Agualar* is titled "How to Avoid Injury From Crocodiles." The writer's first suggestion: Stay out of the water. A swimming or wading human is no match for the aquatic croc. The Agualaran caiman is twelve feet long, weighs more than two hundred pounds, and can swim up to fifteen miles per hour. It lunges at twenty miles per hour. If you *are* in water, however, when the croc attacks, smash the end of its snout with your fist. The blow will stun the beast long enough for you to swim ashore. Once on shore, the writer says, no worry. Stand very still, your hands raised above your head. On land, the crocodile can't turn on its side. And since its jaws open only one way, straight up and down, the flat, thick, horizontal reptile will have nothing to grab on to. Unless you have incredibly knobby knees or something. A color photo shows an attacking caiman, its powerful jaws gaping open toward the camera, sixty needlelike teeth shining in the tropical sunlight. I guess the *Manual* is helpful if you plan on swimming in a river. Too bad the *Manual* didn't include instructions on how to deal with other unpleasant creatures. Like extremely rude paleontologists with bad hair.

"You can't tell him about the crocodile," said Jared.

"But how else are we going to get under his tent?" asked Uncle Stoppard.

"Why can't we tell him, Jared?"

"Because he'd go and tell the Ackerberg guys," said Jared.

"So?"

"Aren't they supposed to be coming through here one of these days? They might come tomorrow," said Jared.

"They might not," I said.

"The point is, Freaze might mention it to them, and then the Ackerbergs would simply dig up the crocodile themselves. No thank-yous. No reward."

Jared had a point.

"We have to dig it up first," I said. "Quick."

"Maybe if we discussed it with Tulsa Freaze," said Uncle Stop.

Jared removed his cowboy hat and scratched his head. "Nope. 'Cause he'd tell his dad."

"It's not fair," I said. "It's our crocodile. Not theirs."

"It's not ours, Finn," said Uncle Stoppard.

"It's not the institute's, either!" I cried. "Not really."

"No, but it was part of the original Zwake discovery. Which is why I think the institute might pay us, would pay us, in place of your parents. But only if we turn the crocodile over to them ourselves."

I could imagine Einstein Head handing over the golden crocodile to one of those black-suited, black-gloved creeps. And then getting a nice fat reward. Our reward. Why would he need any more money? He's already famous. He's already got the Ackerbergs paying him, buying him fancy equipment.

"What if they accuse you of holding out on them?" asked Jared. "Like, why didn't you tell them about the gold when they came to Minneapolis?"

"We didn't learn about the crocodile's existence until later," said Uncle Stoppard.

"Think they'll believe you?" said Jared.

"It's the truth," I said.

"Yeah, buddy, but people don't always believe the truth."

"Does that mean we have to lie?"

"We don't have to lie," said Uncle Stoppard.

"Then how are you gonna get under Freaze-boy's tent?" said Jared.

"We'll dig a tunnel," I said. "Just like a Paziosaurus."

"You mean a Tuscanosaurus," said Uncle Stoppard, smiling.

"Can you believe those two guys, two grown men, arguing over what to call a dead animal?" said Jared.

"They'd be famous," said Uncle Stoppard. "Their names would be in the history books."

"And on the Internet," I said.

"They'd be asked to write books and articles, asked for interviews on talk shows, speak at colleges, get funding for future projects—"

"Money, huh?" said Jared.

"Big money," said Uncle Stoppard.

"All for some big, dumb lizard that died a million years ago."

"Sixty million years ago," I said.

"Back to the crocodile," said Uncle Stoppard. "Any ideas?"

Even in the shade the air was hot. It was hard to

think. Across the dusty road from us, on the other side of our parked car, insects buzzed and hummed in the tall grass. Buzz and hum. Maybe we could use the mechanized Arm to lift Professor Freaze's tent while he was sleeping. No one would hear it.

"Anyone see you making your map, Finn?" asked Jared.

"Huh? I mean, yeah. All of them saw me. Except Nixon. He's lying down in Dr. Himmelfarben's tent." I wondered if it was as hot inside those high-tech tents as it was on the desert highway leading to Chuca.

"Tell the scientists you're curious about your parents."

"Which I am."

"Which you are. Tell them you're trying to find out as much as possible. Especially since they've been gone for so long. And tell them you think your parents buried something in the ground. Tell them there was a thief at the Zwake dig."

"Which there was," I said.

"Which there was. And say that your dad buried something underneath his tent for safekeeping."

"All of that's true," I said.

"Just don't tell them what your dad buried," said Jared.

"What if they ask?" said Uncle Stoppard.

"Lie."

A car engine roared to life. One of the campsite's black Jeeps rocketed past us, shooting up clouds of choking dust from the road.

"Who was that?" asked Uncle Stoppard.

"Looks like that Zé fellow," said Jared. "In a real big hurry."

"Zé!" I turned and saw Fleur Freaze. She was waving her arms, trying to get the Jeep's attention. Too late. It was swallowed up by walls of waving grass and billowing orange dust.

"Everything all right?" asked Jared.

"What? Oh, yes," Fleur said. "I mean, no. Nothing is all right. My father-in-law just fired Zé Mirón."

"What?"

"And he fired Mr. Paz, too." Fleur pulled a handkerchief from her pocket and wiped the back of her neck.

"Can he do that?" asked Uncle Stoppard.

"He just did," said Fleur. "I saw the whole thing."

"But weren't you all hired by the Ackerbergs?" said Uncle Stoppard.

"Oh, my goodness. I forgot all about them. They usually come here once every month, and they're long overdue this time."

"Will Professor Freaze hire more people?" asked Jared.

"I doubt it," said Fleur. Then her face grew bright red. "In fact, the old buzzard said he'd fire me, too. If I wasn't family. As if that means anything to him."

"How can you keep working?" asked Uncle Stoppard. "There are only four of you left."

"Maybe you'll have to quit and go back home," I suggested.

"Actually there are five, counting Mr. Wu," said Fleur.

"He's going to work with you?" said Uncle Stoppard.

"My husband convinced his father that Mr. Wu held valuable information concerning the underground tunnels. At first, the professor disagreed. You've seen for yourself how he can be with people. But then the old man gave in. Now he talks as if recruiting Mr. Wu was his idea."

"So Nixon is staying?" I asked.

Fleur nodded. She jammed her hands into the pockets of her khakis. "Professor Freaze thinks that Mr. Wu and the Arm are the only extra help that he needs. He sometimes acts as if Tulsa is in the way here, too. Well, anyway, tomorrow morning José and Gabriel are leaving. It will be so quiet around here without them. And without another woman to talk to—"

"What do you mean?" said Uncle Stoppard.

Fleur sighed. "Dr. Himmelfarben has decided to leave as well. She hasn't told Professor Freaze yet, but she saw him arguing with Zé. Heard him fire the two men. She told me she was quitting. Said she'd been thinking about it for the last few weeks. Said she's never seen such unprofessional behavior. The two of us were talking when I heard Zé getting into the Jeep."

"The doctor's right," said Jared.

Fleur flashed a look at him.

"Sorry about that," he said.

"No, that's all right," she said. "And I certainly can't blame Dr. Himmelfarben. Professor Freaze is—well, lately, he's been impossible. I know he's always been a bit difficult to work with, but now this!" She shrugged her shoulders. "I better get back to Tulsa. He's writing up a report for the institute."

"Um, where's Mr. Paz?" I asked.

"I don't know," said Fleur. "Walking around somewhere. Maybe down by the river. If I know him, even though he's upset, he's probably spending his last afternoon here digging around for more of those—those stupid eggs!"

Her eyes were wet with tears.

"This is all because of that ridiculous curse!" Fleur turned quickly and ran back to her tent.

7
The Curse Returns

The Curse of the Zwakes was back.

Seven years ago the curse had doomed the campsite of my mom and dad. Priceless Mayan artifacts were stolen. Aunt Verona disappeared. She reappeared days later, only to vanish once more over the thundering waterfall at the mouth of the Pellagro River. My dad had to identify the broken body pulled from the wreckage of his sister's canoe. Hurricane Midge forced my parents to flee and abandon their work. Then they evaporated among the volcanoes of Iceland. This last summer the curse reappeared in Minneapolis. A man was killed because of the same golden treasure my parents had unearthed in Agualar. Another man was stabbed. Uncle Stoppard fell off the roof, got beaten up by two nurses, and was attacked by a ski pole (although he didn't know at the time it was a ski pole). I almost became breakfast for a family of ravenous raccoons. And another woman, an evil woman, met her death in a second, furious waterfall.

As soon as Fleur ran off, I looked over at Uncle Stoppard. He had a strange light in his eyes. Was he thinking the same thing? The curse had returned to Agualar. Because I, another Zwake, had returned, misfortune would pounce on the campsite faster than a tropical storm. Zé and Gabriel Paz lost their jobs. Dr. Himmelfarben was abandoning Fleur. Would something worse happen?

"I'll bet that dinosaur now will be named the Tuscanosaurus," said Jared.

"Let's get out of here," said Uncle Stoppard.

Not out of Agualar, just out of the camp. Uncle Stoppard drove us over to a restaurant in Chuca called El Dedo de Oro—The Golden Finger. Paintings of Agualar's famous cacti covered the outside of the low brick building. Inside, the restaurant was only as big as our living room back home. I felt as if we were eating in someone's house. One wall was painted with more golden cacti and dancing women in green and pink. Old movie posters (*Jaws 2, The Poseidon Adventure, Saturday Night Fever*) hung on another wall, alongside advertisements for big bars of yellow soap. Over our table glowed a *Madonna*, a framed painting of the Virgin Mary, surrounded by burning roses and fat baby angels. She looked hot and sad.

The restaurant's single room was lit by one large bulb dangling on a cord from the center of the ceiling. Whenever someone opened the door, the draft would blow the lightbulb back and forth. The shadow of Uncle Stoppard's nose swung back and forth like a pendulum across his chin. Sizzling sounds, spicy odors, and laughter drifted from behind a brightly striped curtain at the end of the room. The Chucan food was good—enchiladas, rice, stuffed peppers—but the place was like an oven. Only one full day in Agualar, and already I was sick of my clothes sticking to my body like plastic wrap.

Jared learned from our waiter, who spoke only Spanish, that the magic show was gone. The traveling carnival had moved on to Juanpablo.

"Maybe we can drive over there tomorrow night," said Uncle Stoppard. Juanpablo, ten miles away, was where Jared's gun was being protected by the bald, mustached cop and his partners.

"I've never seen a magic show before," said Jared.

"Uncle Stoppard," I said. "Are we ever going to dig up that golden crocodile?"

"Not so loud, Finn! We don't want the whole town hearing about it."

"That's all we need," said Jared. "More treasure hunters."

"If Professor Freaze can fire those guys," I said, "does that mean he can order us off the campsite, too?"

"Look." Uncle Stoppard pointed toward the front door. Fleur and Tulsa Freaze had stepped inside and were peering around. Tulsa saw us first and waved. Fleur walked over, smiling. She looked a lot happier than she did earlier in the day. "We picked up a few supplies," said Fleur. "And we're also looking for Zé. He hasn't come back yet."

"Maybe he went to see the magic show," I said.

"Those enchiladas look yummy," said Fleur.

"Care to join us?" said Jared.

Tulsa shook his head. "Thanks, but we ate before we drove into town."

"More apple strudel?" said Uncle Stoppard.

"Wiener schnitzel," said Tulsa. "I keep telling Dr. H. that we can trade off and take turns cooking, but she always insists."

"I must have put on ten pounds since we've been down here," said Fleur, patting her flat stomach.

Maybe that's why Zé was avoiding the campsite. Cuisine à la Himmelfarben.

"We need to check a few more spots," said Tulsa. "If you see Mirón tonight, you might mention we were looking for him."

"Will do," said Uncle Stoppard.

After they left, and once the shadow of Uncle Stoppard's nose had stopped swinging again, I said, "Do you think the curse did something to Zé, too?"

"There is no curse," said Uncle Stoppard.

"The curse didn't fire those guys," said Jared. "Some jerk professor did."

"Maybe the professor's not that bad," said Uncle Stoppard.

"Not that bad?" said Jared.

"Maybe those guys caused problems. Maybe he really can find all the dinosaur eggs he wants using only the Arm thing. We don't know. He's rude, yeah. But we don't know everything about those people."

"Especially Nixon," I said.

"Yes, especially him."

"Fleur seems nice," said Jared.

"She seems lonely," I said.

"Tell you what," said Uncle Stoppard. "Let's go back to camp and play some backgammon. I'll bet that by tomorrow morning things will have calmed down and Professor Freaze will be in a much better mood."

Maybe by yelling at Zé and Gabriel Paz, Professor Freaze got the poison out of his system. Like one of those Agualaran scorpions mentioned in the trusty

Manual. Tomorrow he would be calmer, easier to talk with, happy to let us dig under his tent. His hair might even be combed.

"Tomorrow I want to see inside that trailer," I said. If I lived to see tomorrow. On the way back we were almost run off the road by a huge black truck. The guys in the truck made impolite gestures and swore at us. Uncle Stoppard said it was a good thing I didn't understand Spanish.

Jared gritted his teeth and said, "Yeah, but I do."

Tulsa was right about the morning coming early in Agualar. After a few games of backgammon, I slipped inside my sleeping bag, blinked my eyes, and boom! The sun was lighting up the eastern walls of our cozy, blue hexagon. Uncle Stoppard said the fresh, country air made him sleep like a log. The three of us ate breakfast by ourselves that morning: grilled cheese sandwiches, bacon, and powdered doughnuts that Jared bought last night at the Chucan combo store (Uncle Stoppard said it was "one half gas station, one half hardware, and one half groceries"). We washed it all down with lukewarm orange juice.

What were the dinosaur hunters eating? Their breakfast table looked crowded. I noticed that Zé's Jeep was parked next to the campfire.

Fleur jogged over while I was brushing my teeth. She was wearing green hiking shorts, a short-sleeved yellow blouse, and a tan baseball cap. Everyone in camp wore a hat of some kind, even me, to shade our eyes and keep the boiling sun off the tops of our heads. "Still want to see that surprise?" she said.

We followed her to an aluminum, egg-shaped trailer

parked on the far side of their camp where Dr. Himmelfarben, Gabriel Paz, and Nixon Wu stood waiting.
Nixon was leaning on a slim wooden stick as a cane.
Wasn't Gabriel Paz supposed to be gone this morning?
The trailer resembled a small motor home, with wheels,
windows, an extra tire mounted on the back, and a single side door. The license plate said: DINOX. Dino eggs.
Fleur unlocked the door and led us inside. The seven of
us crowded around a metal table at the back of the
trailer. The table was covered with four or five intriguing humps, each covered by a clean white cloth. Fleur
lifted one of the cloths.

A person standing outside of the trailer must have
thought fireworks were shooting off inside. "Oooooh.
Aaaaahh." Nixon Wu was extremely impressed.

A fossilized dinosaur egg, smooth and round, lay before us. Nine inches long, five inches thick, and tapered
at one end, the egg was almost perfect. A thin crack
crawled up one side and widened as it zigzagged over the
top of the egg. At the crack's widest spot a small sharp
rock jutted out from the egg at a steep angle. No, not a
rock. It was a beak. From a hatchling dinosaur. The baby
Paz, or Tusk, or Genus Indeterminata (that's what was
handwritten on an index card lying next to the egg) had
begun breaking out of its shell when the Death Star
crashed into the Gulf of Mexico and smothered it in
mud.

"Are we the first people to see this?" I asked.

"Among the first," said Fleur. "Only the people in
camp have seen this."

"And the institute," said Dr. Himmelfarben. "We send
them photos by computer."

Tulsa popped his head inside the trailer. "Fleur, do you have the keys for the Arm?" he asked.

She shook her head. "Your father was the last person driving it."

Tulsa mumbled something and then took off.

"So well preserved," breathed Nixon Wu, lightly fingering the crack in the shell. "Are these all eggs, too?"

"No," said Fleur. "And that's the surprise for Mr. Zwake here."

That's when things started to get really weird. Fleur lifted another cloth. Lying on the table, mere inches from the egg, was a gleaming golden knife with feathers carved into its handle.

"Mayan," I said.

Dr. Himmelfarben nodded. "When we dug it up last week, we were certain it must have been part of the original dig years ago. Part of the Zwake find. But it was wrapped in a plastic bag and buried only a few feet below the surface."

The knife was a foot long and looked exactly like other artifacts I had seen in my dad's old photographs. This was part of the curse.

"Inside a plastic bag?" asked Nixon Wu.

"Dr. Zwake told me that several artifacts had been stolen from the site," said Uncle Stoppard. "Maybe this was one that—"

"That the thief buried," I said.

"The thief?" said Fleur.

"Why would a thief do that?" asked Gabriel Paz.

"Uh, that way, um, no one would find the knife in her, or his, tent. Or wherever they slept. You know, no incriminating evidence."

"That's one possibility," said Dr. Himmelfarben, staring at Uncle Stoppard.

"And when everyone left camp for good," I continued, "the thief could come back later and dig up her loot. His loot. Their loot."

"So there might be more than one plastic bag?" said Nixon. Nixon Wu was too smart. If he kept asking questions, he'd learn the real reason for our visit to Agualar.

A man screamed. Tulsa.

"He needs help," said Jared.

We all ran outside. Fleur paused a second to lock the door behind her.

"There," said the doctor. Tulsa was standing next to a tent, waving his arms.

By the time we reached him, Zé was standing there, too.

"What is it?" asked Fleur.

Tulsa was breathing hard. He pointed to the tent. "It's Dad," he said. "I think he's dead."

"Where is he?" asked Dr. Himmelfarben.

"Still inside," said Tulsa. "It's all locked up. I, I don't have a knife—"

The black tent sat ominously still. The door flap was zipped and locked from the inside. All the window shades had been zipped down as well.

"Then how can you tell?" cried Fleur. "I mean, if you haven't been inside. Did you hear him? See him?"

Tulsa led us to the back of the tent. One small corner of the back window's inside flap had caught on something, providing a small triangle to peek through. Fleur bent down and stared through the gap. She quickly stepped back. "Oh my God!"

Everyone else took their turn to look. I squeezed next to Uncle Stoppard and peered into the dim interior of Professor Freaze's tent. A dark figure sprawled on a cot in the middle of the tent. It was the professor, lying face-down. A gleaming knife protruded from his back. A golden knife with feathers carved into the handle.

8
Impossible

Jared used his Swiss Army knife to slice a long vertical slit along the eastern wall of the tent. He pulled apart the two new flaps and stepped inside. He had talked Tulsa Freaze out of ripping open the front entrance. "Fingerprints," said Jared. "We don't want to disturb the evidence."

"Evidence?" gasped Fleur.

"It's murder," said Nixon Wu. "No man can stab himself in the back."

If any man could, I wouldn't put it past Professor Freaze.

I stood next to Uncle Stoppard just outside Jared's new entrance. Nixon stood on the other side of the slit. Everyone else gathered quietly around the cot in the middle of the tent. It was dim inside; the morning sunlight was blocked by the other tent next door. Tulsa and Fleur's.

"Jared," said Fleur, "are you sure that all the zippers are locked and snapped in place?"

"It seems so, ma'am," he said.

"How could someone get in here?" asked Tulsa.

"More important," said Dr. Himmelfarben, "how could someone get out?"

The high-tech Ackerberg tent was completely closed up from the inside. All the snaps were in place. The zippers were zipped. The entrance lock was locked. Whoever had stabbed Professor Freaze would still have to be inside, but that was impossible. The tent was too small to hide anyone. The only other objects in the professor's tent besides his cot were some average-sized suitcases, piles of folded-up clothes, a lantern, a stool, and a small metal table covered with notebooks and a laptop computer. The computer was plugged into one of those fancy outlets sewn into the fabric of the tent. Under the cot lay a pair of the professor's dirty socks.

"It's impossible," said Fleur.

"That can't be the knife we were all looking at just a moment ago," said Jared. Tulsa reached for the golden handle, when Jared backed him away. "Fingerprints," he said.

"Here," said Dr. Himmelfarben. She grabbed what looked like a big handkerchief off the Professor's table and reached for the blade.

"A moment," said Gabriel Paz. "He could still be alive." Paz leaned over the body, laying a hand on the side of the Professor's neck. Yuck! His tie flopped down and landed on the reddish stain in the Professor's back. Seconds later he straightened up and looked over at Tulsa. "I'm sorry," he said.

Nixon tipped forward around the tent flap to get a better look. He lost his balance, lost his cane, and fell half-in, half-out of the tent. I helped him to his feet. "Sorry, about that," he said.

Dr. Himmelfarben gently pulled the knife out of the professor's back, using the handkerchief to preserve fingerprints. Then she held it out toward Jared. I couldn't believe it, it was the same knife.

"I don't believe it!" cried Fleur. She ran out of the tent and raced toward the egg trailer. I followed her. She unlocked the trailer door, threw it open, and dashed inside. I found her staring at the metal table that held the baby dinosaur egg and the mysterious humps beneath their white cloths. She flung off all the cloths, revealing more fossilized eggs. The knife was gone.

"Help me look for it," she said. Fleur crawled beneath the table. I made sure the knife wasn't lurking under a discarded cloth. We looked in cabinets, under chairs, behind cushions, inside the small bathroom. The knife was no longer inside the trailer.

Fleur stared at me with frightened eyes. "How could Professor Freaze be stabbed with that knife? We all saw it just a minute ago?"

"And how did it get inside the tent?" I asked. A locked tent.

"It's the curse," said Fleur.

"My uncle says there is no curse," I said.

"Then how do you explain all those disasters that happened at your parents' dig? That woman falling over the waterfall? And all the things that have been happening here? The ghosts—"

"Ghosts?"

"Well, *spirits* is what the locals call them, but it's the same thing," said Fleur. "That's why we weren't able to hire any local workers. They were afraid of the Mayan spirits. Said they could see them at night, bands of them floating through the air, like the ancient warriors."

"Have you seen them?" I asked.

"No, but I have noticed things moved around."

"Like what?"

"Oh, the mechanical Arm is not always parked where we left it at night. Sometimes the breakfast table is moved. I can see drag marks where the table legs have been pulled across the ground. Sometimes people's boots are missing, or are set in front of someone else's tent."

"Wow."

"And sometimes supplies are missing. Not big things, little things. Like an extra pair of work gloves, or a pair of pliers, or the foam."

"Foam?"

By this time we were outside the trailer. Fleur had locked it up again and pocketed the key. A few wooden crates were stacked up behind the trailer. Fleur lifted the lid of one of these, revealing a pair of green metal cylinders. They looked like the helium tanks you see at stores that are used to blow up birthday-party balloons. "It's chemical foam," said Fleur. "We use it to pack the eggs and anything else we might find out here. It sprays, like a fire extinguisher. And the foam hardens, forming a protective layer. It's actually very useful. The Ackerbergs thought of everything."

What would the Ackerbergs think of Professor Freaze's murder? Would they order the paleontologists back home?

"You're from the United States, right?" I asked.

"Yes. Tulsa and I and his—father—were—are—from Arizona. So is Dr. Himmelfarben. Zé is from Mexico, and Gabriel Paz comes from Ecuador."

"No one's from Agualar?"

Fleur shook her head. "The curse. All the Agualarans

we spoke with were afraid to work here. After what happened seven years ago."

Back at the tent Fleur stepped inside to join her husband.

Uncle Stoppard stepped out and crinkled his green eyes at me. "Where did you go?"

I explained that Fleur and I searched for the Mayan knife back at the trailer.

"We were all looking at that knife just minutes ago," said Uncle Stoppard. "I don't see how it's possible."

"Maybe there are two knives," I said.

"Back in the trailer they said this was the only one they found."

"Maybe a second one was found later. By someone who didn't want the others to know."

Everyone began exiting the professor's tent. I noticed blood on the cuff of the doctor's long-sleeved shirt from when she had picked up the knife. That impossible knife. Gabriel Paz had a weird-looking stain on the end of his tie. Fleur was crying on Tulsa's shoulder.

"Where's Jared?" I asked.

"He drove over to Juanpablo," said Uncle Stoppard. "To notify the police. Um, excuse me, Dr. Himmelfarben, but you said you sent a picture of that knife to the institute."

She nodded. "We send them photos of everything we dig up."

"Do you still have those pictures on disk?" asked Uncle Stoppard.

"Yes, we do. Why?"

Uncle Stoppard told the doctor about my theory of a second knife. "If we examine the knife that killed Professor Freaze, and compare it with the photo on the computer, we can see if they match."

"You think there are two separate Mayan knives?" asked Tulsa.

"We only found one," said Zé.

"It's physically impossible for one knife to be in two different places," said Uncle Stoppard. And yet, I thought, that's what appeared to have happened.

"But we'll have to wait until the knife returns," he said.

"Where is it now?" I said.

"Jared took it with him to police headquarters. He was worried about it being tampered with if he left it behind."

When the Juanpablo cops arrived, they did not look happy. The bald cop, we learned his name was Sergeant Eneas Diego, followed Jared inside the dead professor's tent. Five minutes later, when they came out, Sergeant Diego looked much happier. Jared looked upset. The cops piled back into their car, waved at Uncle Stoppard, and disappeared down the dusty road.

"What was that all about?" asked Dr. Himmelfarben.

"Are they coming back?" asked Gabriel Paz.

Jared sat down on a camp stool outside the professor's tent. "No, not for a while."

"Don't they want to investigate?" I said. "They have to find out who killed Professor Freaze."

"They say it's outside their jurisdiction," explained Jared.

Tulsa exploded. "Outside their jurisdiction? I don't believe this! This is impossible!"

"Now, darling," said Fleur. "Calm down."

"None of us is Agualaran," said Jared. "And the local

police don't want to get involved in the murder of a famous American scientist."

"So, no one cares what happened to my father?"

"Calm down, Freaze. Your father's death will be investigated," said Jared.

"Yeah? By who?"

"By me."

9

Prisoners

"No one can leave the campsite," said Jared.

"What!?" (Everyone said this.)

Jared stood up from the stool. "Not until the murderer has been found," he said. He pulled out his badge and flashed it to everyone. The dinosaur hunters hadn't known that Jared Lemon-Olsen was a cop.

"Not all of us are Americans," said Gabriel Paz. "Why should we be forced to remain here?"

"Because an American has been killed, and you all work for an American-based operation."

"Not me," said Zé. "I've been fired."

"You still can't leave," said Jared. "The police are giving all of our names to the border guards. And they'll be driving by here at least once a day to check up on us."

"*Ridiculo!*" cried Zé.

"I'm going to have to ask you all for your passports," said Jared. "Don't worry, I'm only hanging on to them until we sort this thing out."

"You're not getting mine," said Zé.

"Fine," said Jared. "But you're not going anywhere, either."

"Who's gonna stop me?" he said.

"Please, Mr. Mirón," said Dr. Himmelfarben. "Let's not make this any harder on ourselves."

"What about supplies? Food?" said Fleur.

"Since I've been deputized, I can drive into Chuca for you," said Jared. "Or you can come with me, a few at a time."

"So the police are assuming that one of us killed my father," asked Tulsa.

"I'm assuming it, too," said Jared.

"But why would any of us want the professor dead?" asked Fleur.

"I don't know," said Jared. "But why would a perfect stranger want him dead?"

"Maybe someone came into camp from outside," I said. "A thief."

"Like the fellow who buries things in plastic bags," said Nixon Wu.

"We would have heard someone, Finn," said Uncle Stoppard.

"Maybe not. We were all asleep. You sleep like a log, remember? Maybe their car was quiet. Like the mechanical Arm. You can hardly hear that when it's moving. Or maybe they walked into camp."

"So, why was Professor Freaze's tent singled out?" asked Jared.

"You're asking a kid these questions?" said Tulsa. "My father's death, murder, whatever you want to call it, is serious business. This is not some computer game."

"Stoppard and Finnegan both helped me with a murder investigation back in Minneapolis," said Jared. "I take anything Finn says seriously."

"So you people have been involved in a murder before this," said Tulsa. "Very interesting."

"Why don't the police think you're involved? That you killed the professor?" asked Fleur.

"I didn't know him," said Jared.

"I didn't know him, either," said Nixon Wu. "I just arrived yesterday."

"Yeah, you did, didn't you?" said Tulsa.

"What's that supposed to mean?" said Nixon.

"And you just happened to stumble onto the dinosaur cavern that we've been searching for for months. Just happened to find a sinkhole."

"Those sinkholes are everywhere," said Nixon.

"Lucky you," Tulsa growled.

"Settle down, people, " said Jared. "Settle!"

"What do you suggest we do?" said Dr. Himmelfarben. "Professor Freaze was the supervisor of this team."

"And now I'm in charge," said Tulsa.

"Just because you're a Freaze?" said Zé.

"I don't care who's in charge of your operation," said Jared. "But I'm in charge of finding the murderer. Continue on with your regular work, Doctor. Just don't leave the campsite. Everyone—and I do mean, everyone—stay out of the professor's tent."

Jared took off his straw cowboy hat and wiped the sweat from his forehead with his arm. My T-shirt was already sticking to my back.

"Excuse me, again, Mr. Lemon-Olsen," said Dr. Himmelfarben.

"Yeah?"

"It will start getting very hot soon. It's already quite warm. And Professor Freaze's body, well . . ."

"The trailer," said Fleur quietly. "It has an air conditioner."

Jared looked at her. "Thanks, Mrs. Freaze. Uh, I'll have someone help me with the professor in a few minutes."

Fleur nodded. Tears trickled down her cheeks. She held tightly on to Tulsa's arm. Her husband had grown quiet, rigidly staring into space. "Come on," she said, turning to him. "Let's go for a walk. Oh, here, Jared. Here's the key to the trailer."

Jared examined the key. "This the only one?"

Fleur glanced quickly at her husband and then back to Jared. "Yes. The only one."

While the dinosaur hunters each drifted off separately, Jared asked Uncle Stoppard to accompany him inside Professor Freaze's tent. I went with them. I figured another pair of eyes would be helpful. Especially after what Jared said about me. And also since Uncle Stoppard sometimes has a way of missing what's right in front of his aquiline nose.

The tent had grown warmer. Professor Freaze had not moved. Other than the dark reddish-brown stain on the back of his nightshirt, he might have been taking a siesta.

"There's something very familiar about this," said Uncle Stoppard.

"Yeah, we were just here," I said.

"No, something else, Finn. Something weird."

Jared unwrapped a small bundle on the metal table. It was the Mayan knife. He had placed it there during his brief consultation with Sergeant Diego.

"How do you think it happened, Stoppard?"

"Finn has a theory," said Uncle Stop. "Maybe there are two knives. And this one just looks like the knife we saw in the trailer."

"Dr. Himmelfarben is going to check her photo of the knife," I said. "Then we can tell if it's the same one or not."

"It doesn't explain how the knife, any knife, got in here in the first place," said Jared.

"The killer brought it with him," I said.

"Or her," said Uncle Stoppard.

"And where did the killer go?" Jared asked.

We all turned to stare at the windows and the front entrance flap. Zippered, snapped, and locked.

"The killer should be a prisoner inside the tent," said Jared.

"Could someone zip the front door closed from the outside?" I asked.

"Try it," said Jared. He opened up the front entrance for me.

Standing outside the tent, I could reach inside and pull down the zipper with my hand, but not all the way to the ground. I would need a special tool for that. Maybe a hook, or a long wire.

"And how would you lock the zipper once it was all the way down?" said Jared.

Uncle Stoppard and I studied the locks. You didn't use a key on these special Ackerberg-designed locks. Instead, you twisted shut a small turn-lock, like the kind you sometimes see on women's purses. Or on those lockers you rent at the airport. The turn-lock twisted a full 360 degrees in order to be locked. How could that be done with a wire? The turn-lock was solid. Did the killer use a magnet? No, the locks were steel and nickel. It said so, right on the bottom of the lock.

"Once you figure out how to lock that from the outside," said Jared, "then tell me how you also zippered and locked the extra web-lining just inside the door."

The door zipper locked at the bottom. The web-lining locked at the top.

"Maybe the thief used a knife like you did, Jared. And then they sewed the hole back up again."

"That's not such a crazy idea," said Jared. "It wouldn't take a big hole for someone to wiggle their way inside. Let's check out the walls again."

The heat was beginning to make my eyes water. Or maybe that was the smell. I carefully ran my hands all over the eastern side of the tent, keeping my eyes peeled, or I should say, my fingers peeled, to detect any bumps or seams in the fabric.

"Pay attention to the edges," said Jared. "Where two or more sides come together."

Uncle Stoppard was standing by the back window. "Look at this," he said.

Someone had taped the back window flap to itself, forming a small, triangular peephole. The peephole we had all stared through from the outside.

"This is not good," said Jared.

"Why tape?" I asked.

"Because there's nothing here for the fabric to catch on," said Uncle Stoppard. "And the killer wanted to make sure that we would see the Professor was dead. Omigosh."

Uncle Stoppard dropped onto the stool next to the table. The color drained from his face.

"Is it the enchildadas?" I said.

"Now I know why all this looks so familar," he said.

"Why is that?" said Jared.

"Because I've already killed someone like this," said Uncle Stoppard. "I know how it was done."

10
Cold Clues

Uncle Stoppard's hero, the rival detective of Mona Trafalgar-Squeer's own hero, Revelation-of-St.-John Bugloop, is a cool, quiet guy called Inspector Cold, an ex–college professor and ex–Navy Seal, who once taught chemistry and physics. Cold haunts the Upper Peninsula of Michigan, prowling the small towns and fishing villages and islands of lakes Michigan and Huron. In each book Cold uses his precise knowledge of science to solve the crime and catch the cold-blooded killers. In *Cold on the Carpet*, for example, the murder victim is found stabbed in the back, lying on a carpet inside a locked fishing cabin on Whitefish Bay. All the windows and doors are locked from the inside. All the window shades are pulled down, except for one which is taped open by the killer. Taped open! The killer wanted the police, and especially Inspector Cold, to observe the dead victim before entering the room.

"Because," explained Uncle Stoppard, who was telling the plotline of *Cold on the Carpet* to Jared, "the killer wanted people to see that the victim was indeed dead. Dead inside a locked room from which it was impossible to escape."

"And why is that?" asked Jared.

"So that instead of looking at the simple facts in plain view, the detectives would concentrate all their efforts on trying to explain the impossible. How did a killer leave a room that was locked and sealed from the inside?"

"Well, how did he?"

"He didn't," I said.

"He was hiding?" asked Jared.

I looked at Uncle Stoppard before I answered. I didn't know if I should give away the ending of the mystery before Jared had a chance to read it himself. Uncle Stoppard hates that, but this time he merely nodded.

"The killer wasn't hiding. He was in plain sight," I said. "He was dead."

"You mean—"

"It was suicide," said Uncle Stoppard. "The man stabbed himself."

"The victim was this really mean guy—"

"Like Professor Freaze," said Jared.

"Yeah, sorta," I said. "And he's dying of an incurable disease. And he wants the cops to blame his sons for his murder so they won't inherit his money. Anyway, he makes the suicide look like a murder. He hangs a heavy knife from a thread attached to the center of the ceiling. A fuse wire runs from the floor up to the knife thread. The evil guy lights the fuse with a match, and then lays down on the carpet."

"Cotton thread burns like a fuse, too," said Uncle Stoppard. "The flame eventually reaches the knife thread, burns through it, releasing the murder weapon to plunge into the man's back."

"Pretty cool," said Jared. "Didn't the inspector notice the match?"

"It's mixed up with other matches and cigarette butts in an ashtray," I said. "Inspector Cold eventually realizes there are more matches than cigarettes in the ashtray. People usually use just one match per cigarette. And the matches are different."

Jared stared at the space directly over Professor Freaze's lifeless body. "Are you saying this is a suicide?"

"No, not a suicide," said Uncle Stoppard. "But it does make you wonder why the window was left deliberately taped open. Is this murder so simple that we can't figure it out because we're too distracted by what seems an impossible crime?"

"It's the curse," I said.

"There is no curse, Finn."

"Then how did that knife get from the trailer to the tent? And Tulsa saw the knife in his dad's tent at the same time we were looking at it in the trailer."

"It's impossible for a physical object to be in two places at the same time."

"Unless it's haunted," I pointed out.

"Maybe it's like one of those wormholes," said Jared. "The knife slipped into another dimension."

"Or it was half-in and half-out of two different dimensions," I said.

"A wormhole," said Uncle Stoppard slowly. He returned to the back window and peered closely at the window netting. "Maybe this flap was taped open for a different reason," he said. "Think you can stick anything through there, Finn?"

The netting is called mosquito netting for a reason. Not even an insect can pass through its fine mesh.

"No," I said. "Not even, hey, yeah. A thread!"

"Exactly. Just like—"

"Like *Cold on the Carpet!*"

"A knife could be suspended over the body, from that lantern there, perhaps, and then the thread could pass through this window, through the netting, without making a hole."

"You wouldn't need to burn the thread," I said.

"Right, Finn," said Uncle Stoppard. "You could just pull the thread back through the window after the knife was released."

"And how would you release the knife?" said Jared.

"Um, maybe a slipknot?"

"You were never a Boy Scout, were you, Stop?" said Jared. "A slipknot? There would have to be some thread still attached to the knife."

"The killer pulled it off," I said.

"Who was the first person in the tent?" asked Uncle Stoppard.

"Me," said Jared. "Then Tulsa, then Paz."

"Nixon never went inside the tent, did he?" I asked.

"Wouldn't Professor Freaze see a knife hanging there that night?" said Jared. "He wasn't blind."

"Perhaps it was disguised. Or hung out of sight."

Disguised? Jared grabbed the bloody white handkerchief and hefted the knife in his hand. "Hmm, it's heavy, but not extremely. Hard to call. If this knife fell onto the professor, it might bounce off, or it might make a deep wound. Depending on how hard it hit him."

"The skin on your back isn't real thick," I said.

"True, bud, but you got some bones back there, too. And some pretty thick muscles. Huh, just as I thought, no thread attached, either."

"How long do you think the professor was dead?" said Uncle Stoppard.

"Help me flip him over," said Jared.

Once the professor was lying faceup, Jared examined his eyelids, jaw, and neck. The skin was tight and blotchy. The white Einstein hair stood out like snow from the purplish skin. "Watch this," said Jared. He pressed his forefinger on a spot by Professor Freaze's collarbone. Nothing. "Normally when you press your finger against your skin, it blanches, gets white," said Jared. "And then the blood rushes back and the skin returns to its normal color. Well, judging by the stiffening of the body, and the livor, it looks like—"

"You can see his liver?" I asked.

"*Livor* means 'purple,'" said Uncle Stoppard.

"Actually, it means 'lead-colored,'" said Jared. "But, yeah, I mean the bluish-purplish tone to his skin. Looks like he's been dead at least six or seven hours."

Dead or not, his hair looked the same.

"Killed in the early morning," said Uncle Stoppard.

"I think so. But we really need an expert medical examiner, and I don't think they have one in Juanpablo."

"What are those bugs doing?" I asked. A miniature cyclone of insects was swirling above Professor Freaze's bluish-purplish nose. And above his stiff, open mouth.

"Oops, forgot about that," said Jared. "Let's hustle old Freaze over to the trailer."

They lugged Professor Freaze, cot and all, to the other side of camp. Inside the trailer, they placed his body on a small couch, covering it with a sheet I carried over from his tent.

Uncle Stoppard looked out through one of the trailer's windows. "Nice. They have their own generator. I wondered how they were able to use computers."

"It's not that cool in here," said Jared. "But it's a lot better than being left outside."

"With the bugs," I said.

"Yeah, the bugs."

Jared explained that when any animal dies, including a human being, a certain odor is released from the body. The odor acts like a dinner bell for insects. Flying, crawling, creeping creatures all come to the feast, licking their tiny chops. Professor Freaze's body had been relatively safe until Jared had cut his way into the tent. After that, he was a seven-course meal just waiting for the dinner guests.

"Let's go back, " said Uncle Stoppard. "There's one more thing I want to check."

Now that the professor's cot was folded up and stacked outside the trailer, Uncle Stoppard could investigate the center of the tent. He pulled the stool to the middle of the tent floor.

"Careful," I said. "Your ankle brace came off just last week, you know."

"I know, I know."

Uncle Stoppard had fallen off the roof of our apartment building while researching his next mystery novel and wound up spraining his left ankle. He was trying to climb up to the second floor using a fishing pole. I better not explain the whole plot because Uncle Stoppard hates that.

Standing on the professor's stool, Uncle Stoppard poked his nose around the electric lantern that hung from the center ridgepole. He ran his hands along the ceiling fabric. He waved his arms about, hoping to catch the remains of an invisible thread.

My attention was fixed at the other end of Uncle Stoppard. Below his yellow hiking boots, below the four legs of the stool, and a few feet beneath the tent floor slept the golden crocodile. The thousand-year-old *crocodilo de ouro* that Dad had unburied and reburied, and that had drawn us back to Agualar like a magnet. Does gold give off an odor like a dead body? Will other humans be drawn to this spot, sniffing at the ground and dreaming of treasure? Now that the professor was gone, I mean, transferred to the trailer, there was no reason for us not to start digging.

Odd. Something else was gone, along with the professor. His dirty socks were missing.

11
Getting the Picture

"Forget about his socks," said Jared after I mentioned the missing items. "My gun is gone!"

"Your gun?" said Uncle Stoppard.

"I thought the cops had it," I said.

"They gave it back to me back at headquarters. When I explained the situation, about Freaze's death, they thought it would be a good idea for me to take it. Especially since Diego wants me to produce the killer."

"Where did you put it?" said Uncle Stoppard.

"Right between these two piles of clothes. I walked in here with Diego. Set the knife down on the table. Placed the gun by those clothes. I didn't want anyone to see it if they came in here. And I didn't feel like showing it to the scientists. For security. I didn't want anyone to know that I had a gun."

Too late.

"Everyone was told to stay out of this tent," said Jared.

"They must have come in when we moved Professor Freaze," said Uncle Stoppard.

"Anyone could have done it," I said. "We were gone about ten minutes."

"Even that Wu fellow could have hobbled in here," said Jared.

Uncle Stoppard got down on all fours, his eyes inches from the floor. "So we're missing a pair of socks and a gun."

"Why socks?" asked Jared.

"Maybe the killer hid something inside them," I said.

"Ouch!" Uncle Stoppard sat back on his feet. He reached up and pulled something off his nose. "A splinter!" he said.

"Weird splinter," said Jared. "It looks more like a needle."

It looked like the bristle I had pulled from my foot the first night we got here.

"I'd say it was a cactus needle," said Uncle Stoppard, "but there aren't any cacti around here."

I hadn't realized that before. The campsite forest had lots of trees, and bushes and thick grass, but no Golden Finger cacti.

"Back to your sock question," said Jared. "Why would the killer take them off?"

"Maybe," said Uncle Stoppard, sitting up on his knees, "the socks belonged to the killer."

"Why would he take them off?" said Jared.

Uncle Stoppard shrugged "Who knows? Perhaps it's part of the trick. The method the killer used to kill the Professor and then vanish without a trace."

I was becoming more convinced that the killer did use a wormhole. If wormholes open and close, maybe the hole closed more quickly than the killer planned, and his socks were skimmed off his feet as he plunged into the other dimension.

Jared pulled a thin plastic packet from his back pocket. A portable fingerprint kit. "I got this from the cops, too," he said.

"Don't powder the knife yet," said Uncle Stoppard. "I think our first priority is determining whether there are two separate knives."

"That would simplify the problem," said Jared.

"We need to find Dr. Himmelfarben and look at that computer of hers."

We found Dr. Himmelfarben seated outside her tent at a long white metal table. She was fiddling with the knobs on a microscope. The table was covered with dozens of smallish, squarish plastic containers. Each square held a sample of dirt.

"May I help you gentlemen?" Her Tyrannosaurus smile looked tired. "Ah, you're here for my passport."

"We were wondering about that photo you took of the knife," said Uncle Stoppard.

"But first, I have a question," said Jared. "Did you notice anyone going into the professor's tent?"

"I think I went to bed before he did."

"No, I mean right now. After I told everyone to stay out."

The doctor looked shocked. "Heavens, I was sitting right here and I didn't see a thing."

The new entrance, that Jared ripped in the side of the tent, was in the wall facing away from the doctor. Anyone stepping inside would be hidden from the doctor's point of view.

"Could we see that photo?" said Jared.

"Come inside," said the doctor. " I've got my computer right here. Let's see, I think this is the correct disk."

After a minute of whirring and clicking, the computer screen was overspread with a geometric quilt of small, colorful images. Each image was numbered and labeled. The doctor ran her knobby finger across the columns and rows. "Yes, this is it." She shifted her mouse and clicked on a tiny photo. The quilt was immediately replaced by a full-screen image of the Mayan knife.

"That's it, all right," I said.

"This photo is taken from directly overhead. I believe Professor Freaze took the photo himself. Do you have the actual knife with you?"

Jared unwrapped the golden blade and set it next to the computer.

"Quite intriguing," said Dr. Himmelfarben. "That scratch on the right side of the blade. It's on the photo as well."

"And that feather carved into the handle," said Uncle Stoppard. "Can you enlarge this?"

"Certainly," said the doctor. The mouse clicked, and the virtual knife blew up five times larger. Uncle Stoppard frowned at the two knives, the virtual one and the actual one. His cucumber-green eyes got that squinty, serious look. He sighed. "It's the same one," he said. He tapped the computer screen. "See how part of the feather is rubbed off? It's the exact same way on the pic and on the real knife. Too much of a coincidence for two knives to look like that."

"I'm sorry," said the doctor. She looked up at Jared. "Or should I be?"

"It does make our investigation a bit more complicated," said Jared.

Something bothered me about the Mayan knife. Not just the picture, but the real knife. They looked exactly the same, but I was puzzled. "How could Mr. Freaze, Tulsa, I mean, be looking at the knife in his dad's back at the same time we were looking at it in the trailer?"

"Doesn't make sense," said Uncle Stoppard.

"Unless you believe in other dimensions," I said.

"Here's my passport," said the doctor. "Do you really think the police will force us to remain here, Mr. Lemon-Olsen?"

"I'm afraid they will, Doctor. Unless we find the killer."

"Or come up with an alternative solution," said Uncle Stoppard.

"Alternative?" asked the doctor.

"Was Professor Freaze depressed about anything?" asked Uncle Stoppard.

"Depressed? Oh, no. He was frustrated about not finding the egg cache, of course, but—you think he may have killed himself? That's impossible."

"It's impossible for a killer to vanish from a locked tent," said Jared.

"I mean that Professor Freaze was not like that," said Dr. Himmelfarben. "I'll admit, he could sometimes be rather irritating, but he was a marvelous scientist. Intelligent. Strong-willed. Certainly not one to take his own life. You should ask his son."

"I've got it!" I said. "The knife wasn't really in the trailer."

"It wasn't?" said Uncle Stoppard.

"Did you touch it?" I asked.

"No."

"None of us touched it," I said.

"I've touched it," said the doctor.

"I mean, while we were all crowded around the table. Did you touch it this morning?"

"Well, no—"

"We just looked at it," I said. "What if the knife was a hologram?"

"You mean, like a 3-D projection?" said Jared.

"Uh-huh. We just *thought* it was there."

The Tyrannosaurus grinned. "I'm afraid we don't have that kind of equipment here at the camp. Cameras, yes, but no projectors."

"How could a 3-D image of a knife make that cloth look as if it was truly covering it?" asked Uncle Stoppard.

"The cloth could be scrunched up. Or have wires running through it to make it stiff."

"You have a very imaginative nephew, Mr. Sterling."

"I'm afraid he gets it from me."

"I'm surprised at how cool it is in here," said Jared.

"Amazing, isn't it?" said the doctor. "Some space-age fabric designed by the institute. It keeps us relatively cool during the day and warm at night. I'm afraid I don't quite understand how it works. Chemistry and thermodynamics are not my specialty."

"It's plants, right?" I said.

"Extinct plants, yes. Paleobotany."

"Like me," said Fleur, appearing at the tent's entrance. "I saw you walking over here and remembered you needed our passports. These are mine and Tulsa's."

"Thanks," said Jared.

"I would have come over sooner, but I was helping Tulsa with the Arm."

"Is he gone then?"

"He and Mr. Wu drove over toward the river. They're

still trying to find the entrance to the underground cavern. How are the slides coming, Doctor?"

"Slow, but steady," said Dr. Himmelfarben. "I was starting to prepare the frass."

Frass. Bug poop.

Uncle Stoppard cleared his throat. "Mind if I ask you a favor, Mrs. Freaze?"

Fleur looked a little frightened. She readjusted her ponytail through the back of her baseball cap. "Sure," she said.

"Would you accompany us to the professor's tent? We want to make sure that nothing was taken."

"You mean stolen?"

"We just want to make sure," said Uncle Stoppard.

"We could use your help, too, Doctor," said Jared.

Back inside the Death Tent, Fleur glanced nervously around. "Hmmm, I don't think anything is missing. Wait. His radio is gone."

"Radio?" said Jared.

"He had one of those radio-cassette players. You know the kind that runs on batteries, or you can plug it in? The last time I was in here, I noticed it sitting on his table. He always listens, uh, listened to the local weather stations. He was worried about hurricanes. Since those terrible landslides last year in Honduras. Actually, Professor Freaze had a fear of thunderstorms. I think it was the only thing that frightened him."

Dr. Himmelfarben was standing by the back window. "Fleur, come over here. Why is this taped open?"

Fleur shook her head. "Jared, did you see this?"

"We think the killer did it," said Jared. "Please don't touch it."

"It proves someone else besides Professor Freaze was inside the tent," I said.

The doctor had moved over to the small metal table. She leaned over some notebooks, careful not to touch them. "There may be something else missing here," she said. "The Professor's notebooks are all numbered. But Notebook Number Three isn't here with the others."

"I think he gave that to Zé," said Fleur.

"Did either of you see anyone come in here this morning?" asked Jared.

Both women shook their heads.

"Can you think of any reason why someone would want Professor Freaze's socks?" asked Jared.

"Socks?"

"They're missing from this morning."

"I saw them," I said. "They were lying under his cot. Right there. And now they're gone."

"Maybe someone accidentally kicked them," said Fleur.

"We've searched the tent," Uncle Stoppard said.

"I don't see how a pair of socks can be important."

"Then why would someone steal them?" I asked.

12
Like Magic

Nixon Wu was the only person in the camp who needed a pair of socks. But who would want to slip on an unwashed pair that had warmed the feet of Frizzy Senior? Dr. Himmelfarben must have been struck with the same thought.

"Fleur," she said. "Do you think it's all right to let Nixon borrow some of these clothes? Everything of his was stolen."

"Of course," said Fleur. "I'll help you pick out some things."

"Sorry, ladies," said Jared. "But I need to look through everything first. I'll let you know when I'm through with the clothes."

"Where are Mr. Mirón's and Mr. Paz's tents?" asked Uncle Stoppard.

"They share a tent," Fleur said. "On the other side of ours."

As we watched Fleur and Dr. Himmelfarben walk back to the doctor's tent, we saw Gabriel Paz walking briskly toward us. He was wearing a brown tie and a white short-sleeved shirt with skinny pink stripes. "Excuse me, but I'm behind schedule." He strode right past us. "I have some things to attend to."

"At the trailer?" I asked.

"Where's Zé?" said Jared.

"I have no earthly idea."

"I need to ask for your passport," said Jared.

"So typically American," said Paz. "Wherever you go, you people think you are always the ones in charge." He waved a hand in the direction of his tent. "It is back there, somewhere."

"Are you planning to continue working here, Mr. Paz?"

"I was fired."

"Exactly, so why are you still working?"

We had all reached the trailer by now. "Hmm," said Paz. "I forgot it was locked."

Jared held out the key. "I'll give you this if you'll answer a few questions."

Gabriel Paz folded his arms and stared at Jared. "Very well."

"Professor Freaze fired you," said Jared. "And now he's dead."

"Yes."

"You were supposed to be gone by this morning. But here you are, working."

"As long as I am here, I will work." Gabriel Paz removed his glasses and polished them against his tie. "You think I stabbed Professor Freaze in order to keep my job? This is not the only dinosaur dig in the world, *señor*. Nor is it the only dinosaur dig in Agualar."

"There are more?" I said.

"There are many jobs requiring my particular talents."

"What exactly are your particular talents, Mr. Paz?"

Gabriel Paz reset his glasses. "Provenance," he said.

"Pardon?" said Jared.

"I can look at a shard of bone and tell you whether it came from the fibula of a diplodocus or the nest of a Zigongosaurus."

"That must come in handy," said Jared.

"It's a gift," said Gabriel Paz.

"What's a Ziggy—"

"A Zigongosaurus. May I have that key now? It's very hot out here."

"How long are you planning on staying?" asked Jared.

"In the trailer or in Agualar?"

"You know what I mean."

"I'm staying until you find the murderer. I don't have a choice, remember?"

"Then you go back to Ecuador?"

Gabriel Paz avoided Jared's gaze. "I have not decided. There are many places I could go."

"Does the institute pay well?" asked Uncle Stoppard.

"The Ackerberg Institute pays extremely well," said Gabriel Paz. "Better than any other scientific institution in the world. But I come from a family of importance in Ecuador. The Pazes. A family of high standing. The money does not concern me." Then he added, "As it may concern others."

"Such as—?" asked Jared.

"Speak with the Freazes. If they are honest, they will tell you how the late professor was removed from a dozen universities. Fired. In case you hadn't noticed, he lacked people skills."

"So the guy was rude," said Jared.

"And repeatedly unemployed."

"But the Ackerbergs are paying for this," said Uncle Stoppard.

"So why would the Freazes be concerned about money?" said Jared.

"The Tiresome Threesome have worked several digs before. Digs where they had to come up with the money themselves. Ask Himmelfarben, she knows the score. I don't believe they have finished paying bills for their last three expeditions. May I have the key now?"

Jared handed it over. "What are you working on?"

As he fit the key into the lock, Paz said, "I have to pack some of the dinosaur eggs for shipment."

"With the special foam?" I asked.

"Yes, you've seen it?"

"What foam?" asked Uncle Stoppard.

I described the chemical tanks that Fleur had shown me behind the trailer.

"Return the key as soon as you're finished," said Jared. "I'll be around."

Gabriel Paz stepped inside the trailer and slammed the door. A second later we heard a scream from inside. The door burst open. Paz stumbled out and sat down on the grass. "There's a dead body in there!" he gasped.

"Really?" said Jared. "Diplodocus or Zigongosaurus?"

Gabriel Paz glared at him.

Jared smiled and said, "Please don't touch the professor. Unless you want your fingerprints on the murder victim."

When we reached our tent, Jared sprawled out on the grass and said, "I need a beer."

"It is lunchtime," said Uncle Stoppard, checking his wristwatch. "You're not worried about leaving Paz with the professor?"

"If anything funky turns up with the body, we can always testify that he was alone with the professor for an unspecified length of time. We've got three witnesses."

"When are we going to dig up the crocodile?" I said.

"It's better if we wait," said Uncle Stoppard. "It'll look disrespectful if we head over there now with our shovels."

"I'll bet that Nixon guy has a shovel," I said.

"Don't worry, Finn. We'll get the croc. But we need to let people calm down first."

"We always have to let people calm down. First, we had to let the professor calm down, and he's dead. Now it's everybody else. These people are never calm! I say we dig it up tonight, and then fly back to Minneapolis." And then on to Iceland.

Uncle Stoppard shook his head. "If anyone sees us digging up more Mayan gold, they might report us to the Ackerbergs."

"Why would they do that? Because they're not calm?"

"Because we suddenly lost our welcome," said Jared. "And it's all because of me."

"Just cuz you're a cop?"

"An American cop. And suddenly I'm in charge of this investigation, and everyone feels trapped here."

"Let's blow this place," said Uncle Stop.

"We can't go anywhere," I said.

Uncle Stoppard pointed at the horizontal Jared. "We can go anywhere with the American cop. Let's vamoose to our favorite diner." Enchiladas beneath the sad-eyed *Madonna*. It could be worse. Dr. Himmelfarben might invite us for lunch.

"Before we go, let me get the key from that Paz guy," said Jared.

During daylight hours, you didn't notice the shadows from the Chucan restaurant's swinging lightbulb. The tables in The Golden Finger were crowded with noisy, cheerful customers. These people were not worried about what to name a new breed of dinosaur, or disturbed about a psycho killer slipping in and out of locked tents. They were normal. We got seated at a table with a family of six. I felt something warm against my legs. I lifted up the edge of the bright orange tablecloth and saw a skinny white dog wagging his tail. It was our old four-footed welcoming committee to Chuca. During the meal, the kids in the family kept accidentally dropping chunks of meat and cheese onto the floor. But when we got up to leave, I noticed the floor was spotless. Licked clean.

We stepped out of the restaurant, stuffed like tortillas. I could tell I had grease smudges on my glasses because my sight was slightly blurry. Uncle Stoppard and I both took off our glasses and began wiping them with our shirts. I heard someone say the word "freeze." Then I heard "Professor Freaze." I put on my glasses. No one else was standing nearby. But I recognized the black truck parked across the road from the restaurant. The same truck that nearly crashed into us yesterday.

When we got into the rental car, Uncle Stoppard surprised me by saying, "Let's go see the magic show."

"It's too early," I said.

"Let's drive over and see what time it starts," he said. "Who knows how long they're staying in Juanpablo."

"Sorry, Stop," said Jared. "I need to get back. I really should have a talk with Tulsa before too long. And I need to look for fingerprints. And my gun. You two go by yourselves."

"You're the one who's never seen a magic show before," said Uncle Stoppard.

"I'm sure I'll survive," said Jared.

"If you come with us," I said, "you can get an extra gun from the cops."

"I don't think so, bud. I have a feeling that Sergeant Diego isn't too keen on handing out free weapons to foreigners. Even if the foreigners are police."

Uncle Stoppard and I were soon driving out of camp for the second time that day. Jared waved his cowboy hat in farewell as we rumbled down the dusty road.

Highways are only important for getting into or out of Agualar. Once inside Agualar, forget it. The sign to Juanpablo said it was only ten miles away, but it took half an hour to reach by the winding, bouncing dirt road. Juanpablo was a regular place, meaning it had a grocery store, a magazine store, and a furniture store.

The traveling carnival sat on the eastern outskirts of Juanpablo. It cost twelve *quetzals* to get in, about two American dollars. I was surprised the carnival was open, but the ticketseller said it opened at noon. *"Medio dia."* Middle of the day.

The magic show, which played five times throughout the *dia,* was supposed to begin in a few minutes. We sat with a hundred other people under a red-and-yellow striped canopy, a giant tent without walls. Long, low wooden planks faced a small raised stage at one end of the canopy. Black curtains covered the wall behind the stage. Looking around, I thought I recognized a familiar face in the crowd.

"Is that Nixon Wu?" I said.

"Where?" said Uncle Stoppard. "If it is, he should be back at camp."

A tiny band next to the stage started squeaking out music. An explosion. The magician appeared from a puff of pink smoke. He wore a purple suit and tipped his purple top hat to the audience. His assistant reminded me of Fleur, young and pretty. She had long red hair and wore a sparkly, spangly pink leotard. The men and boys in the audience whistled and hooted at her practically the whole time she was on stage. She flashed her white teeth, but the magician was not pleased. As a magician he wasn't bad. He sawed the girl in half. He levitated her. He placed her in a big wicker basket and stuck it full of swords. She stepped out of the basket, of course, without a spangle out of place. Fishbowls appeared out of thin air, doves flew out of the purple top hat. But the coolest act was the doll.

The magician and assistant rolled a large wooden box onstage. They lifted the lid, pulled out a lifesized rag doll, and plopped it on the stage. Then they pretended to fight over the doll. They yanked it back and forth, they threw it in the air, they twisted it around and around. The magician yelled at the girl, the girl pretended to cry. They each grabbed one of the doll's legs and ran in opposite circles. The little band tooted and drummed, trying to make the fight sound exciting. Up to this point I was actually bored with the whole thing. Then the music stopped, the magician and assistant bowed, and the doll stood up! The assistant reached over and unzipped the doll. It was a costume. Out stepped a young, dark-haired guy covered in sweat. The audience stood on their feet and roared. The sweaty guy smiled and waved.

"Wow! A contortionist," said Uncle Stoppard.

"You mean someone who blackmails people?" I said.

"That's an *ex*-tortionist. This guy is able to wiggle his body into all kinds of shapes."

"Double-jointed, huh?"

"More like triple-jointed. Hey, look."

The crowd had been chanting *Luis, Luis, Luis* (which turned out to be the contortionist's name) until finally the magician walked offstage and returned with a large, clear plastic jug. It looked smaller than the wastebasket in Mr. Thomas's science class. The magician set the jug on a table, tilting open the hinged lid. Señor Luis leaped onto the table. He placed one foot inside the jug, then the other. He took a deep breath and squatted down. His bones must have been rubber. In less than a minute Luis had crammed his entire body inside the plastic jug. The magician slammed shut the lid, and the audience exploded. Adults were clapping and stamping their feet, boys and girls were screaming. Dogs were barking. An older woman fainted. It was the best show I ever saw.

I wanted to get the rubber guy's autograph when the show was over, but he was surrounded by a crowd of giggly girls. I did not see Nixon Wu anywhere. On the way to the car Uncle Stoppard bought us each a cone of cotton candy. And he bought a balloon.

"What's that for?" I said, munching a wad of sticky pink sugar.

"A theory of mine," said Uncle Stoppard. "That fellow back there gave me an idea."

"The contortionist?"

"Yup."

"I'll bet this has something to do with Professor Freaze's tent."

"You'd win that bet."

"So, tell me."

Uncle Stoppard grinned. He likes acting mysterious.

Besides candy and toys, the carnival also sold souvenirs. Like small wooden swords. Conquistador swords. They reminded me of the golden Mayan knife that killed the Professor. What was it about the picture of the knife on Dr. Himmelfarben's computer screen that bugged me? Something looked weird.

As we drove out of Juanpablo, and as Uncle Stoppard behaved like a contortionist himself by trying to eat his cotton candy and steer at the same time, he said, "Okay, grab the balloon from the backseat." So I did.

"Now try to push it with your finger, but not too hard. Don't pop it."

I pushed gently at the surface of the blue balloon.

"I don't get it," I said.

"Now let all the air out." So I untied the end of it. *Pffph. . . .* "Now push the balloon again," he said.

Push it? But it was all limp. "You mean push through it?" I asked.

"Think about it, Finn. It's the same balloon, but it can be either hard or soft."

"Yeah?"

"Flexible. Like the contortionist."

Señor Luis could push and pull his body like a boneless chicken. He crammed himself into that plastic jug without blinking his eye. Did someone in the camp squeeze their way in and out of Professor Freaze's tent? Wouldn't it take a person with special talent to do that?

I knew Uncle Stoppard wouldn't tell me the answer until he could show the stupid balloon to Jared. Hmm, was a balloon part of the trick?

It was dark when we arrived back at the campsite. A strange car was parked next to our tent. The license plates were from the United States.

As we stepped out of our car, Jared ran up to meet us.

"Careful, Stop," he said. "Those Ackerberg guys are here."

13
Institutionalized

"Visitors to the Agualaran forests," says the trusty *Manual,* "should not be surprised at encountering panthers, boa constrictors, or venomous scorpions." I hadn't encountered a single dangerous creature. Not until that evening. The deadliest animal had just arrived by automobile. A pair of them had arrived, in fact. One black, one white, both male, both bald. I recognized their familiar protective coloring: black suits, black gloves, and black sunglasses. Sunglasses at night? More protection, I thought. If you can't see their eyes, you can't know what they're thinking.

Should I be grateful to the Ackerberg Institute for giving my parents work? My dad and mom never had to worry about money, according to Uncle Stoppard. But the institute was also responsible for sending my parents to Agualar, where the curse began. And for shipping them off to Iceland. Did the institute know where my parents were now? Did these two particular Ackerbergers know that I was the son of the famous archeologists, their two former employees, Leon and Anna Zwake?

They knew a lot more than I realized.

Uncle Stoppard stepped out of the car and was stopped by the black Ackerberger. "Where is the golden crocodile?" he said.

I must have had a funny look on my face because the Ackerberg guy looked at me. I mean, his head swiveled in my direction. I couldn't actually see his eyes, because of the sunglasses. But I could feel him staring directly through my eyeballs and into my brain. Think good thoughts. Think good thoughts.

"Crocodile?" said Uncle Stoppard.

The black man reached into a coat pocket and produced a photo. "The golden crocodile," he repeated. I stretched my neck to get a glimpse of the photo. It showed my mom and Aunt Verona, smiling, holding a small Mayan figurine between them. *Crocodilo de ouro.*

"I'm sorry," said Uncle Stoppard. "I've never seen that before." That was the truth, too. "And I don't remember that item being on the list your people gave me." Uncle Stoppard reached into his khakis and produced his own sheet of paper. It was the original list the other Ackerberg employees (at least I don't think it was these same guys) had given him when they unloaded our storage locker back in Minneapolis.

Uncle Stoppard and the Ackerberger stood staring at each other, not flinching, not breathing. The whole country of Agualar stopped breathing. Even the insects in the tall grass stopped buzzing.

The Ackerberger stuffed the photo back inside his coat. "I understand there is an investigation," he said.

Jared interrupted. "I explained about the murder, Stoppard. The institute people have been talking with me and Tulsa about his father's death."

"Unusual circumstances," said the Ackerberger.

"Very," said Uncle Stoppard.

"Not unlike one of your own mysteries, Mr. Sterling."

"You know me then? I'm flattered. And you are—?"

"Call me Mr. Black." The Ackerberger motioned for his companion to join them. "And this is also Mr. Black." The white Mr. Black nodded.

The black Mr. Black continued. "We check in with the Freaze team at least once a month, monitor their progress, handle any difficulties that may arise."

"Difficulties," echoed the white Mr. Black.

"It is unfortunate about Professor Freaze's death," said the black Mr. Black. "He was a great scientist. His contributions to the institute and the world will certainly be missed."

"I'm sure," said Uncle Stoppard. I peered over at the dark campsite. Where were the living scientists? Hiding in their zippered, snapped, and locked Ackerbergian tents?

"His death is unfortunate for another reason, Mr. Sterling."

"And what reason is that, Mr., uh, Black?"

"The Freazes are frozen. The team's work is now hampered by the police."

"Not exactly hampered," said Uncle Stoppard.

"They are not free to come and go. Their passports have been confiscated. Their supplies have been tampered with."

"Supplies? Well, this is the first I've heard of it," said Uncle Stoppard. He looked over at Jared. "Have you heard that?"

Jared shook his head.

I remembered what Fleur told me in the egg trailer, just after we discovered the professor was dead, while she and I hunted for the Mayan knife. Ghosts, she said. Spirits floating among the trees. Supplies disappearing, like work gloves and the special chemical foam.

"Mr. Black, I realize that the investigation is, well, inconvenient," said Uncle Stoppard. "But I'm sure you've spoken with the Freaze team. I'm sure they want to discover who killed Professor Freaze just as much as the Juanpablo cops do."

The Juanpablo cops didn't seem wildly enthusiastic about catching the murderer. Especially since they expected Jared to do all their work for them. I'll bet they'd be looking for suspects if one of their precious cacti had been killed.

"And we're not in charge here," said Uncle Stoppard. "We're just visiting."

"But I'm in charge of the investigation," said Jared.

"Officer Lemon-Olsen, you know nothing about the golden crocodile, either?" asked the white Mr. Black.

"Uh—"

A siren screeched through the night. Headlights bounced along the dirt road and approached the campsite. Sergeant Diego and his men jumped out of their car.

"Señor Black," said Sergeant Diego. They had met before? How did the cops know the Ackerbergers were here? I noticed a cell phone in white Mr. Black's hand.

The Agualaran cops and the two Mr. Blacks conversed rapidly in Spanish. Jared and Uncle Stoppard and I looked helplessly at each other. Why didn't they include Jared in their conversation? Who was in charge here? The huddle broke apart. Sergeant Diego and the muscle-builder cop approached Uncle Stoppard.

"I am sorry, Señor Sterling," said the Sergeant. "But I am placing you under arrest for the murder of Professor Freaze."

My heart stopped.

"You're joking," I said.

"Diego, you can't do this!" said Jared.

"Death is no joke, *muchacho*. Señor Sterling was not honest about his reasons for coming to Agualar."

"What do you mean?" asked Uncle Stoppard. "I'm honest."

"He means this," said the black Mr. Black. From another pocket he produced the map Uncle Stoppard had drawn yesterday, showing the outlines of the former Zwake campsite. The fat red X marking the location of Professor Freaze's tent stood out on the paper like blood.

"A detailed map of Professor Freaze's tent," said Mr. Black.

"No," said Uncle Stoppard. The muscular cop was handcuffing him. "That's the old Zwake site. That's where we were planning to—"

"Planning what, Mr. Sterling?"

"Um—"

"Diego," said Jared, "I thought you told me to handle things. Not these guys."

"Careful, Officer," said the black Mr. Black. "Or you may be charged with withholding evidence."

"What evidence?" I said.

Mr. Black smiled. The black one, I mean. "The Juan-pablo police are avid mystery readers, as I guess you al-

ready know, Mr. Sterling. And they are familiar with
your work. They are now extremely familiar with one
particular story of yours." He pulled a paperback out of
another pocket. *Cold on the Carpet.* How many pockets
did this guy have?

Jared placed a hand on Uncle Stoppard's shoulder.
"Diego, you don't honestly believe Mr. Sterling had
anything to do with—"

"The police deal in facts," said the black Mr. Black.

"This is all circumstantial," said Jared. "Stoppard had
no reason for killing Freeze."

"No reason for wanting Professor Freeze removed
from his tent?"

"Well, removed, maybe, but definitely not killed."

"Just a difference in words," said the black Black.

"You can come down to the station," Sergeant Diego
said to Jared. "We can talk there."

Uncle Stoppard was hustled into the backseat of the
squad car. Two cops squeezed in on either side of him.
"I'll be fine, Finn," he said. "Just be sure to—" The door
slammed shut.

"We'll follow in our car, Finn," said Jared.

Where was a cosmic wormhole when you needed
one? Why didn't a monster tunnel open up right now
and swallow the Ackerbergs and the cops? Shoot them
through a million dimensions and fling them into the
middle of a blazing red supernova? And their bodies
would be compressed by the tremendous gravity pres-
sures into nothing but tiny, insignificant nuggets of
human DNA. Reptile DNA!

The drive to Juanpablo seemed to stretch out for a
thousand miles. But I don't remember a single inch. All

I could think of were the cruel, unsmiling, inhuman Ackerbergs. If they hadn't hired my parents to work in Agualar, none of this would be happening. The gold crocodile wouldn't be buried under Professor Freaze's tent. Come to think of it, the professor's tent wouldn't be standing there if it wasn't for the same Ackerberg Institute. They're the reason he was sent here. And if the institute hadn't shipped my parents off to Iceland, Uncle Stoppard and I wouldn't even need to dig up that old statue. We wouldn't need the reward money for plane tickets, and expedition supplies, and Icelandic explorer guides. Because my parents would be home.

The Ackerbergers were experts at taking things away. They took my parents, now they were taking my uncle. Just so some stupid scientists they hired can keep looking for dinosaur eggs and feel free to drive into town for cheeseburgers whenever they wanted. I didn't know what was going to happen next, but I knew one thing. I was not going to calm down.

The Juanpablo police station was cold inside. Cold and ugly. It was four times the size of the Chucan restaurant with squeaky tile floors and wallpaper the color of peanut butter. Jared spoke to the cops while I sat on a sticky wooden bench, watching them fingerprint Uncle Stoppard, remove his wristwatch, belt, and wallet, and drag him through a heavy metal door at the rear of the waiting room. CARCEL said the sign over the door. I suppose the cells were back there.

Jared sat down on the bench.

"Can't we at least talk to him?" I cried.

"Not yet, buddy. Don't worry. We can come back tomorrow."

"Tomorrow! You mean we're leaving him here in this crummy place?"

"We have to, Finn. He's under arrest."

"Uncle Stoppard didn't kill the professor. Everybody back at camp knows that."

Jared shrugged sadly. "Those scientist guys don't know your uncle like you and I do. We're strangers down here. Unknowns. And people have a fear of the unknown. It's a lot easier for Tulsa and the others to believe his dad was killed by somebody else instead of by one of them."

"But one of them did it!"

"Yeah, but which one?" said Jared.

Which one? I could think of at least two. I noticed Zé Mirón was absent from camp. And Gabriel Paz said he didn't know where his tentmate was. Was Paz lying, and was Zé hiding out from the cops? Did Nixon Wu travel halfway around the world just to hunt eggs? Professor Freaze said over breakfast that he remembered Beijing. Maybe the two paleontologists had met before in China. So maybe Wu came to Agualar for another reason. Or was he just a geek, an "egg-hound"?

"This stinks," I said.

"It sure does, buddy."

Stinks like frass.

"Tomorrow I'll see if there's an American consulate nearby," said Jared.

When we drove out of Juanpablo, I saw the strings of red and yellow lights that marked the carnival. What was Uncle Stoppard trying to show me with that balloon? He said it was flexible, like the contortionist. First it was hard, then soft. I told Jared about it on the drive back, but he didn't know what to make of it, either. He said he'd ask Uncle Stoppard about it when we drove back in the morning.

Sergeant Diego and his pals might think the investigation was over. They might think that Uncle Stoppard killed Professor Freaze with a knife and thread like the Whitefish Bay suicide in *Cold on the Carpet*. They were wrong. And Jared and I had to find the real killer before Uncle Stoppard was shipped off to some disgusting wormhole of an Agualaran prison.

The Ackerberg car was gone by the time we got back. Great! Maybe a cosmic hole opened up after all. I noticed Tulsa Freaze sitting at the table by the campfire, a beer in his hand. He seemed to be waiting for us. I hated coming back to camp. Each time we did, something terrible happened. Tonight was no exception.

"We found Zé," said Tulsa. "Inside the trailer. His head was cracked open with one of the eggs."

14
Blood

When I saw the dinosaur egg that had been used to crush Zé Mirón's skull, I felt relieved. Not because Zé was dead, but because I suddenly realized what had been bugging me about the computer pic of the Mayan knife. Dr. Himmelfarben's photo was accurate, it hadn't been faked or tampered with. The weapon that we saw in the trailer was the weapon we saw in the tent. And that's exactly what was wrong.

Since Jared was still in charge of the murder investigation, as soon as Tulsa told us about the second killing, we rushed to the egg trailer. It was late and I was starving, but death is more important than powdered doughnuts.

The campers were gathered outside the trailer. Nixon Wu was leaning on his same old stick. Gabriel Paz puffed on a thin cigar. Wait, Fleur was missing.

"In here!" shouted Tulsa.

The body of Zé Mirón was sprawled facedown across the floor of the trailer. One arm was crumpled beneath him. The other arm, his left, was caught in the sheet that covered the late Professor Freaze. In fact, Zé's stiff hand was grasping the sheet, pulling it off the body, exposing the dark, brownish stain on the professor's back. On top of Zé's skull rested the dinosaur egg. Genus Indeterminata. The fossilized baby's beak was covered in blood. So was most of the trailer. The floor was a dark, sticky pool.

"Who found him?" said Jared.

"I did," said Tulsa. "Right after you and the Ackerbergs left."

"Was anyone else in here?"

"No. I came to use the rest room. Someone was in the portable john, so I stepped in here."

"Wasn't it locked?"

"I got the key from Fleur."

"Fleur? When was that?"

"How am I supposed to know? Aren't you even going to look at the body?"

"I can already see he's dead, Mr. Freaze. And I have a pretty good idea how he got that way. I need to find out who had access to this trailer. Why was Zé even in here?"

"Beats me."

"And how could he even get inside if you had the key?"

Tulsa grew still. "There are two keys," he said.

Jared reached into his pocket and pulled out a key. "This is the other key," said Jared. "I got this from Paz before I went into town this afternoon. So how did Zé get in here?"

"I don't know."

"Why did your wife tell me there was only one key to the trailer?"

"I don't know," said Tulsa. "Maybe she was afraid.

Maybe she thought she was protecting me because she knew I had a key, too."

Jared looked closely at the key in his hand. He leaned out the trailer door and said, "Paz, come in here."

Gabriel Paz shook his head violently. "Not with those two—those bodies—in there."

"When was the last time you saw Mr. Mirón?" said Jared.

"Not since breakfast," said Gabriel Paz. "Then he disappeared."

"Me, either," said Nixon Wu. "I saw him at breakfast, and then I was busy with Mr. Freaze over by the river."

"Dr. Himmelfarben," said Jared, standing in the narrow doorway. "Tulsa said you had an extra key for this trailer." Tulsa was about to protest, but Jared held up his hand. Dr. Himmelfarben could not see Tulsa inside the trailer.

"Yes," said the doctor. She reached into her work pants. "I believe I have it on me."

Jared whistled and then looked back at Tulsa. "Looks like there's a bunch of keys floating around," he said. He held up the one in his hand, the one he had taken earlier from Paz. "This key is a copy. A duplicate. You can see that it wasn't issued with the trailer. All these extra keys were probably made at the hardware store in Chuca." Now I knew why Jared Lemon-Olsen was a cop.

Dr. Himmelfarben looked down at the grass, embarrassed. "It was my and Fleur's idea," she said. "We took the key into town and had copies made. It was always so inconvenient having to hunt down that one key. And you never knew who had it last."

"Exactly how many keys are there?" asked Jared.

The Tyrannosaurus grinned. "Three," she said. "No four. Three copies, and one original."

Jared knelt down inside the trailer and carefully searched Zé's pockets. "I shouldn't be doing this until the body's photographed," said Jared, "but since I'm the only cop here . . . ah, here it is." He fitted a bloody key into the door lock and smiled grimly. "Well, now we know how Zé got in here. And with the door unlocked behind him, anyone else could have easily slipped inside. Where's your wife, Freaze?"

"Lying down in our tent. She's not feeling well."

I was looking at the dinosaur egg, and trying not to look at Zé's head. I was glad his face was turned away. Like the professor's.

"Hey, Jared," I said. "When you and Uncle Stoppard carried Professor Freaze in here, didn't you place him on his back?"

"You're right, Finn. So why's he facing down?"

"Is that important?" asked Tulsa.

"You're the scientist," said Jared. "Tell me why someone would flip over a dead body?"

Tulsa shrugged. "Perhaps when Zé was killed, he accidentally moved the professor as he fell to the floor."

Jared shook his head. "Then the professor would be on the floor, too. But he's still on the couch. Completely turned over. Looking at how Zé pulled the sheet off the body, I'd say the professor was turned over before Zé was killed."

"Maybe Zé did it," I said. "He's strong enough."

"Why?" said Jared.

"Was he looking for something?" I asked. Nothing to

look at but the stain on the professor's nightshirt and the gaping wound in his back. That was it! I looked again at the dinosaur egg, at the dark blood on the miniature beak. At the dark pool on the floor of the trailer. Now I knew why the Mayan knife picture was wrong.

"Two more things, people," said Jared. He had turned out the lights of the trailer and shut the door. We all stood outside on the dewy grass. "This is a murder scene, so I don't want anyone going inside. I'll get the police out here tomorrow. Secondly, my gun is missing."

"Gun?" said Nixon Wu.

"You all know I'm a police officer. Well, my weapon is missing. Stolen. Someone took it after I set it down in Professor Freaze's tent."

"You think one of us has it?" asked Tulsa.

"One of you does have it," said Jared. "I'm just telling you this for your own safety. You didn't believe that one of you could be the murderer. Some of you actually believed that Mr. Sterling was involved. I don't see how he could have killed Mr. Mirón while he was at the carnival today, do you? Someone here killed Mirón. And that someone is armed. Have a good night."

None of the campers said a word.

Under the light of our hexagon-tent's lantern, while plowing through several powdered doughnuts, I explained what I had seen to Jared.

"Blood," I said.

"Blood?"

"The dinosaur egg was covered with it. But the Mayan knife was not."

"Yeah . . . ?"

"When we looked at the actual knife and compared it with the computer pic back at Dr. Himmelfarben's, something about the picture bothered me."

"But they were exactly the same."

"I finally figured out that's what bothered me," I said. "The Mayan knife should have looked different. It should be covered with Professor's Freaze's blood."

"You're right, Finn. If the professor had been stabbed earlier, hours before Tulsa discovered him, the knife should have been covered with dried blood."

"But when Dr. Himmelfarben showed us the knife in the tent, it was clean." I remembered the blade gleaming dully in the dim sunlight.

Jared sat back on his sleeping bag. "So what happened to the blood?"

"Vampires?"

He ignored me. "The professor was not killed with the Mayan knife."

"Maybe he wasn't killed with a knife at all," I said.

"What do you mean?"

"What if he was poisoned? And then, after he dies, the killer sticks the knife in the professor's back to make it look like he was stabbed."

"And throw us off the trail of a possible poisoner? Good idea."

I got it from one of Mona's mysteries that's set in Sea World, *Poisoned on Porpoise*.

Jared groaned.

"What's wrong?" I asked.

"I didn't see any symptoms of poisoning on the professor."

"Perhaps the poison isn't normal," I said. "Maybe it's

from a scorpion or some weird chemical they have down here."

"That's why we need a medical examiner," said Jared. "You know, Finn, even if old Freaze was poisoned, it still doesn't explain how that Mayan knife got into his back."

"But it does prove that something else killed the professor—either poison or a second knife." Or something with a sharp and deadly blade.

Jared turned out the lantern and we both got into our sleeping bags. A few minutes later, I crawled over to my suitcase in the dark. My hand dug through my extra socks and comics and T-shirts and found my small canvas travel bag. I felt a long, thin case. My dad's lucky hunting knife. I shoved it in the pocket of my shorts and crawled back inside my sleeping bag.

15
Down by the River

Early next morning, while sharing a mountain of *huevos rancheros* with the paleontologists, an ancient, beat-up looking *ambulancia* arrived in camp. The bodies of Professor Tuscan Freaze and José Mirón were destined for a bigger city named Zalapa twenty miles on the other side of Juanpablo. Zalapa had a hospital where the autopsies would be performed, and an American consulate that would help ship the bodies back to their respective homes of Arizona and Mexico. Jared had called Sergeant Diego with Tulsa's cell phone, and Diego had contacted the hospital in Zalapa. After the *ambulancia* rumbled off with its cargo, Jared gave me the bad news.

"We can't see your uncle today."

We were sitting in the rental car with the doors open. Jared wanted some privacy from the scientists.

"Why not? What's wrong?" I said.

"Today's some kind of religious festival, and the cops have to be out on the streets all day and all night. To make sure people don't get out of control."

"So nobody's at the jail?"

"Yeah, but Diego won't let me see Stoppard unless he's there, too."

"Doesn't he realize that Uncle Stoppard couldn't be the killer since Zé is dead?"

"Diego's waiting to hear the medical report. He wants to be sure about the time of death."

"It was last night. What more does he need?"

"I'm sure Stoppard will be released soon, Finn."

"Yeah, as soon as everyone's done parading through town."

"I did learn something from the ambulance guys, though," he said. "They're pretty sure Freaze died from the stab wound. It didn't look like poisoning to them."

"So we need to find the real knife that killed him."

"And if knives are anything like keys around here," said Jared, "this place is probably crawling with them."

I reached into my pocket and fingered my dad's lucky blade. "Think of all the sharp instruments and tools and stuff the scientists use," I said.

"One other thing I did while you were finishing up breakfast and cleaning up the tent." Jared pulled out a small notebook. "I established where everyone was last night."

"Trying to find out who could have followed Zé into the trailer?"

Jared nodded. "Everyone has alibis. And everyone was alone. Tulsa was in his tent, writing up a report last night. Paz was in his tent reading. Nixon Wu was sitting by the campfire. Himmelfarben was on her computer. Oh, and look, I found this in Zé's shirt pocket." He held up a computer disk with a penciled "Z" on the label.

"Think it's a clue?"

"Or just part of his work," said Jared. "There's a computer in each tent."

"Where was Fleur?"

Jared glanced at his notes. "Said she went for a walk down by the river. Said this whole murder business is getting to her. I can't blame her."

"Hey, wait a minute!" I grabbed his notebook. "This is where everyone was last night? Right before Zé got killed?"

"Tulsa went into the trailer, found Zé's body, and then yelled for help."

"Just like before," I said.

"And this is where everyone said they were when they heard Tulsa yell."

"Remember why Tulsa said he went in the trailer in the first place?"

"He needed to use the john," said Jared.

"Because someone was in the portable. But according to your notes, no one was using it."

Jared grabbed the notebook back and scanned it. "So Tulsa was lying about the real reason he was in the trailer."

"Or someone else is lying about not using the you-know-what," I said.

"Why lie about that?" said Jared.

"Good question," I said.

"Why wouldn't someone want us to know they were inside the portable? It's not like it's suspicious to be in there. It's natural."

"Unless they were hiding in there," I said. "And were covered in blood."

The portable john was located about twenty yards behind the trailer. It was hot and smelled of urine and chemicals. It was also very clean, no blood anywhere. Jared opened the lid to the seat.

"Gross!"

"It's gonna get grosser," he said. He knelt down and peered into the smelly pit.

"Finn, go and see if Dr. Himmelfarben or Tulsa have anything like a pair of tongs."

"Tongs?" I peered past Jared and saw something glinting against the inner wall. "Is that apple strudel?"

"Finn, just go and find them!"

I returned to the portable in ten minutes. Tulsa had given me a metal instrument called a calipers that the paleontologists used for measuring dinosaur eggs. It looked like a giant bug claw.

"This is the only thing they had," I said.

Jared held the calipers in both hands and reached down into the seat hole of the portable. "I might need your help with this one, Finn," he said. I really hoped he didn't.

"Nope, looks like I got it."

"Do I want to see it?" I asked.

"I think you do."

The calipers held an unusual object in their precise, metal grip.

"Is that a knife?" I said. No, it was a sword. One of the conquistador swords I had seen at the carnival with Uncle Stoppard. Only a foot long and carved completely out of wood, the miniature sword looked more like a dagger. The tip had been sharpened to a deadly point.

Jared took off his cowboy hat, wiped his head and face with a bandanna, and stared at the blade. The tip was stained brownish-red.

"Is this—?"

"It's blood, Finn. Dried blood. I'll stake my ten years as a cop on it."

The weapon used to kill Professor Freaze had been tossed into the portable john. A good hiding place. No one would think to look down there.

"Real smart," said Jared. "If the sword was thrown in the river, it might float and be discovered by someone later. If it was buried, someone might have dug it up. Especially with all the digging that goes on around here."

"I would have burned it," I said.

"Burning takes a while. The killer needed to dispose of the weapon quickly. And going to the john wouldn't arouse anyone's suspicions. Except yours, that is, bud."

"If the killer wanted to get rid of the sword, why wait until last night?"

We were walking back toward the trailer and were just passing the wooden crates that held the chemical tanks. Jared sat down on one of the crates and stared at his cowboy boots. "Why wait a whole day to dispose of the weapon?" he said, more to himself than to me. "And risk having the weapon found."

"Maybe the killer didn't think of the portable hiding place until last night," I said.

He shook his head slowly. "It's too much of a coincidence that the killer would be throwing away the sword just as Tulsa wanted to use the can."

"Think there's fingerprints on it?"

"On the sword? Nah. It'll be clean—in a matter of speaking."

"Now what do we do?" I asked.

"I'm going to sit down and write up everything we know so far. The murders. The locked tent. The keys. The sword. Stoppard's balloon theory."

"Don't forget the socks," I said.

"Right, the socks. And the tape on the window flap. I'm sure I've overlooked something obvious. Something that's floating around in my overheated brain."

Floating. Like the Mayan warrior-spirits, their glittering shields catching the moonlight.

I told Jared what Fleur had said about the ghosts. How the locals were afraid of working with the paleontologists. "I'd be afraid, too," said Jared. "But not of ghosts. Our killer is real flesh-and-blood."

Jared walked over to the campfire to do his thinking, and I headed for the river. I hadn't seen the Pellagro since Jared drove over the rickety bridge the day before yesterday. The natural clearing ended at a wall of thick shrubs with dirt pathways running in between some of them. Once past the shrubs, the pathways slanted steeply downhill. I could make out the sparkling surface of the river about a hundred yards away. The path I took twisted like a snake, curving up and down and around a series of grassy dunes. The dunes were high enough to block any view of the river when the path ran between them, but I could hear the rush of the water grow louder.

Wide tire tracks crisscrossed my path, flattening the grasses into the sand. Probably made from the balloony tires of the Arm. Balloon. Soft, then hard—like the contortionist. Like magic.

I heard music. Spanish-sounding music. A tango?

The music wasn't coming from the direction of the river, but from behind one of the dunes. I crawled up the sandy side of the grassy hill. The music was coming from a small, battery-powered radio. Professor Freaze's radio. Down below the dune, in a small hidden bowl of sand, about the size of the magician's stage at Juanpablo, were two figures dancing. Dr. Himmelfarben and Gabriel Paz. The sky was hazy blue, the sand was Mayan gold. It looked like a scene from a movie.

Dr. Himmelfarben turned her head in my direction. I ducked down behind the dune, but too late. "Young man!" she called. There was no use hiding. I stood up and waved at the two scientists.

"Finnegan," said Dr. Himmelfarben. I took a few unsteady steps down toward the sandy dance floor. "I know what you're thinking. Yes, this is Professor Freaze's radio. I borrowed it."

"You don't need to explain," Gabriel Paz said to her.

"I borrowed it the night before he died. You can ask Nixon Wu. He saw it in my tent."

"We killed him for his radio." Gabriel Paz laughed.

"Please, Mr. Paz. He'll think you're serious. I didn't want to say anything about the radio while we were in the tent," said Dr. Himmelfarben. "I didn't want Fleur to know why I needed it. I was worried she might be upset with me. I guess it's a selfish reason."

"There is no reason for the tango," said Paz. "It just is. Like the sky. The river." He grabbed Dr. Himmelfarben and whirled her around, just as the cassette jerked to an end. The dancers froze.

The doctor looked back up at me, her face bright red. "Would you mind turning that tape over?"

I flipped the cassette and hit the Play button.

"You may tell your uncle and Mr. Lemon-Olsen, if you like," said Dr. Himmelfarben. "Just don't mention it to anyone else, all right?" The Tyrannosaurus shot me a toothy smile and then clutched Paz in a weird, marching dance step.

Why didn't the doctor want the others, especially Fleur, to know that she liked dancing? Who would ever understand adults? Digging for eggs must loosen something in the brain.

I followed the snaky path to the river, the distant tango music drifting over the grassy dunes. When I got back to camp, I would ask Nixon Wu if he remembered seeing the professor's radio in Dr. Himmelfarben's tent.

The path reached the end of the dunes. I could see the Pellagro. Then the sand disappeared from beneath my feet. I had slipped into a wormhole.

16
Down Under the River

"Not all dinosaurs are extinct, you know."

The wormhole—or *cenote*, as Nixon Wu had described it—had deposited me on the floor of a long, low tunnel. I was sitting half-in, half-out of a pool of milky water. More water dripped somewhere off to my right. *Plink, plink.* I twisted around and saw the entrance of the *cenote* thirty feet away, high above me, at the top of a slippery, sandy slope.

"Some of them are alive. Very much alive."

Nixon Wu was sitting on a rock a few feet away.

"What?" I said.

"Birds," he said. "Birds are dinosaurs, you know."

"No, I didn't know that—and where are we?"

"Another *cenote*. I'm sure this tunnel leads to the big cavern I saw several days ago. I'm sure of it. I'm lucky that way. Year of the Rat, you know."

"Rat?"

"My astrological sign," said Wu. "It's a water sign. And a sign of good luck. I'm sure we'll find that cavern. And the eggs."

A drop of water hit my head.

"See?" said Wu. "Water sign." He chuckled. "It's from the limestone. And, of course, the river. It's directly above us."

"The Pellagro?"

"Uh-huh. It's not real deep here. About fifteen feet, I'd guess."

I stood up and wiped my hands on my T-shirt. "Why were you talking about birds?" I said.

"Over there," he said. He pointed to another rocky pool not far away. Three or four long-legged birds were drinking, silently watchful.

"Those are dinosaurs, huh?"

"Oh, no," he said. "Those are *zancudos*. Descendants of the original dinosaurs. But all in the same family."

I noticed a funny-looking hammer stuck into his belt. The metal claw of the hammer was straight and sharp.

"Looking for more eggs?" I asked.

"Always." Wu grinned. "That's another mark of the Rat, you know. We're discoverers."

"How did you get down here?"

"There's another *cenote* over that way." He pointed.

"Can I ask you another question?" I said.

"Look at this," said Wu. From behind his rocky seat he pulled out another rock. No, an egg. Perfectly smooth and rounded like the egg back in the trailer. The shell's surface was uncracked.

"Wow! Where did you find that?"

"In the pool cavern."

"You and Tulsa finally found it?"

Wu smiled. "I found it. Tulsa has no idea where it is. He thinks I'm still looking for it."

"I don't understand."

"There are lots more," said Wu. "I actually pulled this from a nest of seven eggs. Seven—think of it! And seven is a lucky number, you know."

I noticed that Wu was wearing a short-sleeved shirt and khakis that were a little big on him. They must be extra clothes of the professor's. No, the women hadn't removed the clothes from the tent yet. Maybe they were Tulsa's. "Are you ever going to tell him?" I asked.

"You mean, Tulsa? Oh, yes, I'll tell him. But not until I've had a good look around all by myself. That stupid machine of theirs—"

"The Arm?"

"It's too big and clumsy. And it would never fit down here in these tunnels. Americans always believe their technology can solve everything. They have forgotten how to use their noses."

"Noses?"

"Their senses. Their instinct." Wu laughed and the sound echoed throughout the limestone tunnels and *cenotes.* "Want to see something neat?" he said. He didn't wait for me to answer, but stood up, grabbed his egg, and started walking quickly away. I ran to catch up with him. The wading birds scooted to the other side of their pool as we passed by.

Wu never stopped talking. He boasted about the digs he worked on all over Asia. About the fossils of strange prehistoric birds with unpronounceable names that he helped dig out of the Mongolian desert. Extinct birds was his specialty. One of the ancient birds was named after Wu and his father. He chattered on about the religions of the ancient Maya. "They worshipped a great god called the Plumed Serpent. Plumed, you know, like feathers. It was a dinosaur."

Dinosaur? Wu believed that the Mayan traditions went back thousands and thousands of years further than we thought. That the Maya actually *remembered* dinosaurs. And that's why there are carvings of Tyrannosaurus-like creatures on their temples.

"Like the Labocania," said Wu. "Looks like the T. rex, but smaller. It was a carnivore, too. A theropod. They've found its fossils in Mexico."

Did Wu's passion for feathered dinosaurs bring him to Agualar? The tunnel we were walking through grew darker. My sneakers sloshed through shallow water. I put my hands against the sides of the smooth limestone to keep from slipping.

"American scientists are so concerned with becoming famous," said Wu.

As if Wu was not.

A shaft of light pierced the end of the tunnel. Another *cenote*. I could see blue sky through the opening. Fallen rocks and rubble heaped against the curving side of the tunnel made a stairway up to the surface.

My eyes blinked in the hot sunlight. More of Wu's wading birds stood alongside the Pellagro several yards away. Was it flowing the wrong way? Upstream?

"We are on the other side," said Wu. He pointed with his funny little hammer. "The camp is across the river."

Tall dunes stretched along this side of the Pellagro, too. A slight breeze ruffled the grasses. The sun beat down on our hats. I noticed strange markings in the sand around us. Tracks. They looked like the same tracks I had seen over by the dancing duo.

"Did you and Tulsa drive the Arm over here?" I asked.

"No, no. We have only stayed on that side. He is afraid it wouldn't make it across the river. Though I think it is shallow in some spots. With sandbars, you know."

"Is this where you found the eggs?" I said. "Over here?"

Wu chuckled. "They come from far below. Back among the tunnels. I will show you sometime if you promise to keep it a secret."

"I don't know how long we'll be staying," I said. "Uncle Stoppard will be coming back, and then, uh, we'll probably go home."

"What about the buried treasure?" said Wu.

"Treasure?"

"Buried in plastic bags, remember? The Mayan artifacts that your parents dug up? Don't you think there might be more around, like the knife?"

The impossible Mayan knife.

"Nixon, did you see a radio in Dr. Himmelfarben's tent?"

"Radio?" he said. "I don't know. Maybe I did. An American boom box, you mean? Perhaps. I think I did. But you must promise me one thing. You cannot tell anyone about the eggs."

"But won't the others waste a lot of time looking?"

"Promise," said Wu.

The breeze stirred the grasses at my feet. Our twin shadows stretched across the burning sand side by side. I felt a long way from camp. From Jared. The only sounds were the rushing water and the constant buzzing of insects.

"What's that hammer thing you have?" I asked.

"This? A rock hammer," said Wu. "For working with stone."

"Does it come from China?"

"No, it's American," he said. "I always carry it with me. Stainless steel, Neoprene grip, twenty-nine ounces.

Cutting edge, get it?" He juggled the hammer, the blinding sunlight glancing off it. "Promise about the eggs, okay?"

"I promise," I said.

Wu covered the hammer with a tubelike piece of cloth and then tucked it into his belt. "Let's go back."

I glanced once more at the tire tracks as I climbed down into the tunnel. "You know," said Wu, "that Paz fellow isn't very interested in science. Not really. He is very gifted, has lots of book knowledge. But no instinct. No sense of smell."

As we passed below the river, I mentioned what Gabriel Paz had said about identifying dinosaurs by looking at pieces of bone.

"Did he actually say that?" said Wu.

"Yeah. Have you ever heard of a Zigo—"

"Zigongosaurus?" Wu's laughter echoed through the tunnel. "Ha! The Zigongosaurus didn't have a nest. He barely had a brain. The Zigongosaurus laid his eggs in a row along the ground, while he walked."

"Don't you mean, while *she* walked?"

"Now this creature," said Wu, holding up his egg against the dim light. "This creature had a brain. Ah, yes, brave new creature. A new species with eggs and fossilized embryos to prove it. The Chingchiasaurus."

17
The Balloon Trick

On the camp side of the river Nixon Wu showed me another small, climbable well that led easily to the surface. After making me promise a third and fourth time that I would keep his discoveries a secret, Wu disappeared back into the *cenote*. So many things not to tell people. Don't tell Tulsa about the eggs and the cavern. Don't tell Fleur about the doctor dancing. Don't tell any of the scientists about the small conquistador sword. I was getting all the things I wasn't supposed to remember, mixed up with the things I wanted to remember. And who cared what name the new dinosaur would end up with? I was only concerned with one name: the name of the killer. Right now it was Genus Indeterminata. But by the end of the day it would have a real, human name. Speaking of names, the Chingchiasaurus was a cool name for a dinosaur. I thought it was neat that Wu wanted to name the creature after his paleontologist father.

The wind was stronger since my adventure under the river. Huge clouds like pink cotton candy, sailed majestically overhead.

At camp, Gabriel Paz had returned. He was pulling up one side of his tent that had fallen down in the wind.

"Where's Dr. Himmelfarben?" I asked.

"She is a very busy woman," said Gabriel Paz. His blue tie flew around his neck like a twisting serpent.

"I just have a question to ask her."

"I think, young man, that she is finished answering questions."

Finished? "Is she still down by the river?" I said.

"Please, I am busy. And I need to work on my computer before this storm."

"Storm?"

"Look at those clouds. Rainstorm. Maybe worse."

I ran to Fleur's tent. Empty. She and Tulsa must be off egg-hunting with the Arm. I ran over to the trailer. The door was locked. I knocked, but no one answered.

The camp was deserted except for Paz and Jared, who was sitting on a lawn chair next to our blue hexagon.

"Jared!" I gasped. "I've got it!"

"The killer?"

"I know how it was done." Gabriel Paz and Wu had given me the final pieces I needed to fit the trick together. Uncle Stoppard's balloon trick. "And I think I know what happened to Zé, too."

"Jump in the car, Finn. Let's go get your uncle."

"What about the holiday?" I asked.

"Suddenly I feel real religious," said Jared.

Zooming outside Chuca, on the road to Juanpablo, I finally caught my breath. "It's like Uncle Stoppard said, a balloon trick."

"Someone used a balloon to kill old Freaze?"

"No, the balloon's just an example of something flexible. Like the contortionist in the magic show. And like a tent."

"Tents are flexible?"

"The fabric, or canvas walls, are flexible," I said. "When I saw Gabriel Paz trying to put the side of his tent up, it made me think of Uncle Stoppard's balloon. The side of the tent was collapsed. Like an empty balloon. Not tight, like a balloon full of air."

"So someone fiddled with Freaze's tent?" said Jared.

"It's not that hard," I said. "The killer probably unfastened the stakes that slip through the loops on the bottom of the tent. That would loosen the fabric. At least on one side."

"And the knife?"

"That's the tricky part," I said. "I still don't know how the Mayan knife got in there. But I know how Professor Freaze was stabbed. The wooden sword that killed him was placed in the professor's tent *before* he went to bed. Someone slipped in there, without being seen, and hid the sword inside. Probably on the floor, next to the wall of the tent. Then, while the professor was asleep, the killer loosened the tent stakes so the wall would collapse slightly—"

"Like a balloon."

"Yeah, and then he reached into the fabric, picked up the sword, pushed the fabric closer to the sleeping professor, and stabbed him."

"What about blood?" said Jared. "You saw what happened to Zé. And we know there was blood on the sword. Why didn't we see any on the wall of the tent?"

"That's what the socks were for," I said. "I think the sword was hidden inside an old sock. Then when it stabbed the Professor, the blood got on the sock instead of the tent fabric." When Nixon Wu and I stood on the other side of the river, and he slipped his funny hammer into that protective cloth, I was reminded of socks. Socks are good for holding things besides feet.

"That is great, Finn! That explains how he could be stabbed inside a locked-up tent."

"The killer never had to open the zippers or snaps. Once the professor was stabbed, the killer probably waited awhile, then pulled the sock off so the sword would be visible."

"And dropped the sock by the cot. Even if we had noticed the bloody sock on the floor, it would have attracted less attention under the cot than it would if it was found next to the wall."

"We'd just think the killer used the sock to avoid fingerprints," I said.

"Which they did as well," said Jared.

"With the professor dead, and the sock under the cot, the killer pulled the wall fabric back into shape and refastened the tent stakes."

"It's so simple," said Jared.

"I forgot how flexible a tent is," I said. "Until I saw Gabriel Paz working on his. And it reminded me of what Uncle Stoppard had said about the balloon being soft, then hard."

"You think you know what happened to Zé, too?"

I nodded. "I think Zé figured it out. The trick with the tent. And I think he found the sword somewhere. He went into the trailer to check the professor's wound. To match it up with the sword. But the killer followed him inside."

"Maybe Zé sent a message to the killer to meet him there," said Jared. "To confront him. To demonstrate his theory, and then see what the killer had to say."

"Then Zé turns his back to the killer, pointing to the professor's back, and wham! The dinosaur egg comes down."

"Using the egg as a murder weapon certainly shows it was not planned out. The killer had to work quickly."

"Then the killer took the sword," I said. "And ran over to the portable john to throw it in."

"I still wonder why the killer didn't dispose of the sword right away," said Jared.

"For some reason they couldn't," I said.

Jared pulled into the parking lot of the Juanpablo police station.

"Now all we have to figure out is how the Mayan knife got inside the tent," I said.

Jared pulled the car alongside the first cop he saw in Juanpablo and got directions for finding Sergeant Diego. The sergeant and his men were strolling up and down the main street of the town. A parade must have just passed through. Confetti and flowers littered the streets. Groups of people strolled around.

Jared explained my theory to the weary-looking sergeant. Diego got more excited when he saw the sword we fished out of the john. Especially when Jared pointed out that the tip had been sharpened.

At the police station Uncle Stoppard was released into our custody. As soon as he stepped through the heavy metal door under the CARCEL sign, I ran to greet him. "I told you I'd get out of here, Finn," he said, crinkling up his cucumber eyes. "I told you not to worry."

I helped Uncle Stoppard get his wallet and stuff back at the front desk. While he filled out a thousand forms, I overheard Sergeant Diego talking to Jared.

"The medical examiner in Zalapa confirmed that Señor Miron was killed only minutes before Mr. Sterling arrived back at camp from the carnival."

Minutes?

"And I am sure we will find many witnesses who can testify to seeing a tall, redheaded Americano and a young boy at the magic show. Technically, it does not mean that Mr. Sterling is not involved with the murder of Professor Freaze."

"Doesn't it seem unlikely there would be two killers?" said Jared.

"*Si.* All the same you need to remain in Agualar."

Jared stared out through the tall office windows. "Think there'll be a storm?" he asked. The pink cotton candy clouds had thickened like oatmeal, growing darker and greenish.

"You have not heard?" said the bald sergeant. "There is a bad rainstorm on its way here. You do not have a radio back at the camp?"

"We've been busy with other things," said Jared.

"Listen to the radio," said the sergeant. "It is not a hurricane, but who knows? A storm is a storm."

Once we got back to the car, Uncle Stoppard decided to celebrate with a meal of cheeseburgers at a local stand. We each ordered three. Over French fries and burgers and chocolate shakes that tasted funny, Jared congratulated Uncle Stoppard for his idea about the balloon.

"You should hear what Finn has to say about the knife," said Jared.

So I explained about the picture and the knife looking exactly the same. No blood. And Jared explained about Zé's murder and the dinosaur egg and how we pulled the conquistador sword out of the portable john.

"Conquistador sword?" said Uncle Stoppard. "Oops, watch the road."

Uncle Stoppard added chocolate malt stain to the pop stain on his khakis.

"Didn't you see me handing that sword over to Diego back at the station?" said Jared.

"I guess I was busy," said Uncle Stoppard.

"Remember those swords we saw back at the carnival?" I said.

"Yeah . . . swords," said Uncle Stoppard, dabbing his pants with a wad of napkins. "Now, that makes sense. Since one object cannot be in two places at the same time."

"Unless it's a wormhole," I said.

"So this is our problem," said Jared. "Professor Freaze was stabbed with the sword, but we saw the Mayan knife."

Uncle Stoppard slurped up the last of his malt. "Or did we?"

"What do you mean?" I said.

"We saw *a* knife. It was dim inside the tent, remember. And when we looked through that small window flap, we saw a knife sticking out of a body. We didn't really get a good look at the knife until we were inside."

"But it had feathers carved on the handle," I said.

"If the killer used the sword, perhaps they drew a design on the handle to resemble the Mayan feathers."

"Why do that?" I said.

"To throw us off course," said Uncle Stoppard. "Like *Cold on the Carpet*. We got so involved in the impossibility of the situation, we neglected to think who could have killed the professor and why."

"So the wooden conquistador sword was sticking out of the professor when we looked through the window?" said Jared.

"I think so," said Uncle Stoppard. "And when we left the trailer in a hurry, in all the excitement, someone grabbed the Mayan knife without being noticed. The knife was brought into the tent when the killer stepped inside with the rest of us."

Who? Everyone was inside the tent, except for me and Nixon Wu.

"When our attention was turned," said Uncle Stoppard, "the wooden sword was pulled out of the professor and the Mayan knife took its place."

"But when did that happen?" I said.

"There was only one time when we were all distracted. Someone was going to grab the knife when Jared cautioned us about disturbing the evidence. 'Fingerprints' you said. And then Dr. Himmelfarben walked over to the metal table to get a white handkerchief. We all watched her, and while we were distracted, the switch was done."

"Who did it?" I asked.

"The same person eager to grab the knife in the first place."

I had to think back to the scene. "Tulsa?"

"But, Stop, we heard him yelling from outside," said Jared. "He was outside while the rest of us were inside looking at the Mayan knife on the table."

"One person took the knife. Another person made the switch. Think of it," said Uncle Stoppard. "The last person out of the trailer. The person who locked it up. The only person who could pass the knife to Tulsa without attracting any unusual attention."

The only person Tulsa could trust. Fleur.

18
The Sword

The sky was a dark boiling green above the town of Chuca. The streets were empty. I mean, the dirt road was empty. A few stores had their lights on. Jared used the pay phone at the drugstore to call the cops back in Juanpablo.

"Did Diego believe you?" asked Uncle Stoppard as soon as Jared returned to the car.

"Hard to say," said Jared. "But he liked your theory, Stoppard. Those cops are nuts about American murder mysteries. And he said they're analyzing the blood on the sword over in Zalapa. It does make more sense to Diego that Professor Freaze would be killed by someone who knew him, like Tulsa, rather than by a stranger like you."

Tapping at the back of my brain, like Wu's hammer scraping on rock, had always been the question of Why? Why was Professor Freaze murdered? Because he was rude? Because someone wanted his radio? People are killed for smaller reasons than that. But there was Gabriel Paz's story of the Freazes needing money to pay for previous expeditions. With the professor's death, Tulsa and Fleur would probably inherit insurance money. They could pay off their bills and get rid of a jerk all at the same time.

The trees above the site swayed in the growing breeze. Several of the tents were down on the grass, collapsed like punctured balloons. Lights burned steadily through the windows of the egg trailer. As we rolled into camp, Jared slowly parked the car next to our tent.

"Why do we need to stay?" I said.

"We're not staying," said Jared. "We're packing up and getting out of here. We know who the killer is. I mean, who the killers are. We've told the police. They'll find the professor's blood on that sword. Let them deal with it."

"Let's go dig up the crocodile," I said.

"I think we need to warn the others," said Uncle Stoppard.

"Paz and Himmelfarben?" said Jared.

"And Wu," I added.

"I always forget about him," said Jared.

"Their lives may be in danger," said Uncle Stoppard.

"Our lives might be in danger," said Jared. "We need to pack up without arousing any suspicion and clear out of here."

"Well, the storm will give us a good reason for leaving," said Uncle Stoppard. "We'll say we're going to stay at that motel in Chuca."

"What about their passports?" asked Jared.

"What about the crocodile!" I cried.

It was just like my parents. Another storm, like Hurricane Midge, would chase us away without digging up the rest of the Mayan treasure. That crocodile would stay buried for another seven years.

Uncle Stoppard looked at Jared. "Okay," he said. "I'll

go dig under the professor's spot while you two take the tent down. Hand me that shovel in the back. Finn, remain here!"

Uncle Stoppard crept over the dark grass toward the professor's collapsed tent. It sprawled on the ground, like a thick, black oil stain.

"Finn, grab this lamp," said Jared. He handed me the overhead lantern from inside our blue hexagon.

I could barely see Uncle Stoppard's outline against the dark thrashing trees and shrubs behind him. No rain fell. The clouds kept boiling and thickening. Thunder rumbled in the distance.

"Is this a hurricane?" I asked Jared.

"Too fast for a hurricane," he said. "More like a tropical rainstorm. There could still be some damage, though."

"Floods?"

"Hope not. But that's another good reason to get away from the river."

I glanced back over at Uncle Stoppard. He was brighter. The trailer door was open and light spilled out onto the waving grass. Tulsa stood in the doorway. I could tell he and Uncle Stoppard were talking. Oh, no. Uncle Stoppard put his shovel down. He walked over and stepped inside the trailer.

"Jared, did—?"

"Yeah, I saw it."

"Why would Uncle Stoppard stop digging?"

Jared handed me his cowboy hat. "Do me a favor, bud," he said. "Get in the car and lock the doors."

"But—"

"Do as I say."

He pushed me inside onto the driver's seat. "Here are the keys," he said. "Just stay in here and wait for me. Lock the doors, I said!"

I felt cold inside the car even though sweat dripped down my back. I watched Jared crouch down and run over to the trailer. He stood outside and carefully peered through the small windows. He seemed to be standing in one place for hours. Still no rain, and still the green sky grew blacker.

The air was stifling inside the car. I cranked open the driver's window. Even with just shorts and a T-shirt, I felt miserably hot. When was it going to rain? I don't know how Jared could stand wearing jeans in this kind of weather. Or how Gabriel Paz always managed to wear a tie, even in short-sleeved shirts.

That's it! The hot weather. Everyone wore shorts and T-shirts or short-sleeved shirts. Everyone wanted to stay cool. That's why we always wore hats, to keep the hot sun from beating directly onto our heads. But the morning the professor was killed, like every other morning, Gabriel Paz wore a long tie.

When Uncle Stoppard explained how Tulsa switched the Mayan knife and the wooden sword inside the professor's tent, I first wondered where Tulsa would hide the knife. Or Fleur, for that matter. I kept my dad's hunting knife in my pocket, but its case always made a bulge in my shorts. Wouldn't someone see a bulge in Tulsa or Fleur's clothing? The wooden sword was at least a foot long, so it wouldn't fit very easily into a pocket. But a long tie would be the perfect place to conceal a long, narrow object, like a knife. Paz had leaned over the dead body when he took the professor's pulse.

His tie had flopped down onto the bloody back. Without anyone noticing, had he slipped the Mayan knife out of the tie and slipped the wooden sword in? Like a magician's trick. And once the wooden sword was removed from the professor's back, even though most of the blood would have dried, disturbing the wound would be sure to get some sticky blood on the blade. Blood that would leave a weird-looking stain on the end of the tie.

And that's why Dr. Himmelfarben got fresh blood on her cuff when she pulled out the knife! The wound had been disturbed.

Uncle Stoppard and Jared were confronting the Freazes in the egg trailer. They didn't realize they were wasting time. Giving the real killer time to escape.

I refocused my vision. Jared was gone. Was he inside the trailer?

I unlocked the door, jumped out of the car, and ran. As I reached the trailer, I heard thunder close behind me. I turned and saw a black truck driving into camp, the same truck that almost ran us off the road a few days ago. I ducked under the trailer. Flattening myself against the grass, I watched the truck rumble closer, it's headlights scanning the campground.

I felt the trailer jiggling above me. The sidedoor opened with a squeak. I saw Jared's cowboy boots clump down the metal steps from the door. Then Uncle Stoppard's hiking boots. Then another pair of feet. Gabriel Paz? I crawled over toward the door side of the trailer and peeked out from behind one of the wheels.

Dr. Himmelfarben was holding a Smith and Wesson .357 Magnum aimed at Jared and Uncle Stoppard.

The doctor locked the trailer and then motioned the men over toward the wooden crates.

"Open it!" she commanded.

Jared opened one of the lids. Keeping her gun, Jared's gun, still aimed at them, the doctor reached inside the crate and lifted out one of the chemical tanks. She twisted some plastic knobs at the top of the tank and grabbed the hose.

"Now turn around," she said. "Hands behind your backs!"

Uncle Stoppard and Jared did as they were told. Dr. Himmelfarben aimed the hose at their hands and fired. Thick, white foam sprayed on Jared's wrists and hands, hardening in seconds. Then she did the same to Uncle Stoppard's hands. Then she shot the foam all around their arms and elbows, encasing them in the hard plastic gel.

She dropped the tank to the ground and herded them over to the portable john.

"I don't want to have to shoot you," she said. "It was unfortunate about the others. But I didn't care that much for them."

What happened to Tulsa in the trailer? Where was Fleur?

"You won't get past the border," said Jared.

"If you mean because you still have my passport, well, I don't need it," said the doctor. "My colleagues have a new one for me. A new name and a new life."

Dr. Himmelfarben closed the portable's door and then locked it with a padlock. "This will give me just enough time to get out of Agualar," she said.

I heard Uncle Stoppard's voice from inside the john. "What about the storm? What if there's a flood?"

"You know what they say," said the doctor. "I'm sure this will float."

Dr. Himmelfarben jammed the gun into her work pants and ran to meet the truck. I heard her greet the driver in Spanish. Once the truck's red taillights disappeared down the dirt road, I counted to ten and then climbed out from under the trailer.

19
Last of the Wormholes

"Uncle Stoppard! It's me!" I pounded on the door of the green plastic john.

"Finn, get away! The doctor will see you!"

"She's gone," I said. "She drove off in a truck with some guys."

"Unlock the door, Finn," said Jared.

The padlock was thick steel. "I can't. She's got it locked."

"Go get help," said Uncle Stoppard.

"What happened to Tulsa?" I cried.

"He's tied up in the trailer with Fleur. The doctor made me tie them up, then she ran out of rope."

"Go find Paz," said Jared. "Or Wu. Maybe they have keys."

"And you better hurry, Finn," said Uncle Stoppard. "The rain's going to hit any second now."

As I headed toward the two tents that were standing, I stopped by the black oil stain of the professor's tent. Uncle Stoppard's shovel lay abandoned on the grass. The black tent fabric had been pushed aside and a few clumps of dirt were dug out of the ground. That stupid crocodile! I'll bet it was smiling down there inside its plastic bag.

The two tents were empty. Paz and Nixon were not in camp. Of course, the river. Nixon was probably still over there rustling through those wormholes, hunting for more eggs. When the rain fell, would the tunnels fill up with water?

I ran past the wall of shrubs that lined the camp clearing and found my old path. It snaked up and down the dunes. The grasses hissed in the wind. Sand blew off the dunes in thick sheets, slowly smothering up the pathway, bombarding my glasses. I pulled my cap down to shield my face and kept running.

I rushed around a curve of the path and stopped. A body lay sprawled in front of me. Gabriel Paz. Shot in the chest with Jared's gun. A dark, pool covered with a layer of grit spread out from his outflung arms. His tie flapped across his unsmiling face. Green storm clouds churned across the lenses of his glasses like oil.

Did Dr. Himmelfarben do this, too?

After a few minutes I tracked down the *cenote* that Nixon used for getting in and out of the limestone tunnels. I clambered down and started shouting. "Wu! Wu!" Echoes tumbled around me. Bird's wings flapped somewhere in the darkness.

"Nixon Wu! It's Finnegan! I need your help!"

No sound.

I found my way back to the first well I had landed in. I saw the rock Nixon had sat on when he showed me his new Chingchiasaurus egg. The nearby pool was empty. No dinosaur descendants.

"Nixon! There's a storm coming!"

I ran down the nearest tunnel, sloshing through six inches of water. I didn't remember the water in the tunnels being this deep before. Was rain falling on another part of Agualar, filling up the rivers? I had heard about storm surges that preceded a hurricane, huge walls of water that the wind sent gushing forward in the path of the storm. Like the walls of water that Chicxulub sent smashing through Agualar millions of years ago. If another meteor was going to hit the Earth, I prayed that it would hit the black truck.

"Finn! I'm over here!" Tap, tap. Nixon's hammer was banging against a rock somewhere.

The tapping led me to a vast pool glowing with soft green light. Weird rock shapes stuck out of the water like the fingers of a submerged giant. A knobby, bumpy ceiling curved far above my head.

"Finn, over here." I looked up and saw Nixon kneeling on a rocky shelf that projected out over the pool. "Stick close to the wall," he said. "Use those stones for steps."

"But, Nixon—"

"You'll never believe what I found."

The stone steps were slippery, but I eventually reached Nixon's little perch. He was kneeling in front of a bizarre rock formation. No, they were eggs. Six dinosaur eggs sitting in a circle. An empty space showed where a seventh egg should be. These eggs were even more perfect than the one I saw in the trailer. The egg that had killed Zé.

"You see, the Chingchiasaurus laid eggs much like other theropods," he said. "I don't think it was a swimmer after all."

"Nixon! You must come back. There's a storm coming. And Dr. Himmelfarben killed Gabriel Paz."

"Killed him? I don't believe it."

"She's the killer. She shot him, right on the path to the river. And she has my uncle and Jared locked up. We have to help them."

"Where is she now?" asked Nixon.

"Gone. She left the camp in a truck with some other people."

"What other people?"

"I don't know. But we have to hurry."

"You say Paz is murdered?"

"Shot."

A rushing sound made us both turn our heads at the same time. "Is that the river?" I said.

Thunder rumbled above us. The ground shook.

"Let me make a few more notes," said Nixon. "And then we'll leave."

"But there's a storm—"

The rushing sound grew louder.

"Nixon, did you go see the magic show over at Chuca?"

"No, why? Was it good?"

The rocky ledge quivered. Nixon stood up and put his notebook in his shirt pocket. "That is not the river," he said. The limestone tunnel I had followed to the cavern echoed with a loud rumble. As we both watched, a wall of water gushed through the tunnel and roared into the green pool. More thunder shook the rock ceiling above us. The storm had hit.

"How can we get out of here?" I asked.

Nixon turned and pointed his hammer to the other side of the pool. Another tunnel led off into the darkness, but its lower lip was close to the surface of the pool. As the water level rose, the tunnel would also fill with water.

"It's the only other way out," said Nixon.

I started climbing down the other side of the ledge, but I ran out of rocks to use as steps.

"Nixon? What are you doing?"

He was trying to fit a dinosaur egg into his shirt.

"We have to hurry," I said.

Nixon took off his shirt, twisted it around the egg, and quickly tied a knot at each end. "Finn," he said. "Do you think you could carry one of these?"

"No! Now, hurry."

"But there are no more steps down there."

I jumped off the rocks and plunged into the pool. The water was warmer than I expected. The flow of water gushing through the tunnel behind me speeded up my swim to the mouth of our escape tunnel.

"Hurry, Nixon! Just jump!"

"I don't know how to swim," he said.

"You're a rat," I said. "All rats know how to swim."

Nixon gave me a crooked smile and then glanced nervously at the flow of churning water entering the cavern. He cradled the wrapped egg in his arms and then jumped.

It seemed an hour went by. Where was he? The heavy egg must have carried him to the bottom of the pool. Bubbles broke on the surface. "Nixon!" I called. His dark hair sloshed into view.

"Finn!" he yelled.

I sat on the lip of the tunnel and reached out, pulling him from the pool. "I think I hurt my foot again," he said.

"Hurry," I said. "The pool is getting higher."

Nixon nodded, his hair dripping, and followed me, limping, down the tunnel. The tunnel grew darker, but Nixon had a small waterproof flashlight hooked to his belt. Thunder rumbled above us. The sloping floor seemed to be climbing, but the water level was climbing too. In a few minutes the water had reached our knees.

"Now where do we go?" I said. The tunnel ended with three separate portholes, or mouths, leading out of it. "Which one do we take?"

"Look out!" shouted Nixon. I turned and saw a crocodile paddling along the surface of the water. A baby crocodile, only two feet long, but still a crocodile. The little reptile blinked his tiny eyes at me and slid by.

"There," said Nixon. "Follow the beast. Animals have instincts about these things, you know." The croc swam through the center porthole. Nixon quickly followed him, waving his flashlight into the tunnel. I followed Nixon.

The warm water reached my waist. It was hard to walk along the floor of the tunnel. I reached my hands out, and tried to shove myself along the sides of the smooth limestone. Did Paziosaurs or Tuscanosaurs or Chingchiasaurs, or whatever, really slither through these wormholes looking for a spot to lay their eggs?

Nixon stopped. "We must turn back," he said. I looked around him and saw, in the gleam of his flashlight, a mass of rocks and rubble blocking our path. My heart sank like a dinosaur egg.

"We can't turn around," I said. "The rest of the tunnel is underwater."

Uncle Stoppard and Jared were waiting for me, somewhere above me. They were waiting patiently for me to return and rescue them. Now I needed rescuing. The storm must have hit the camp. Was the river rising? Did long, dark watery arms of the river flow over the dunes and the grass, reaching toward the tents and the trailer. Was Dr. Himmelfarben right? Would the portable john float?

The stupid crocodile! The baby one, not the gold one buried in the ground.

"What happened to its instincts, Nixon?" I cried. "That animal didn't know where it was going. Some nose!"

Nixon aimed his flashlight above us. "Look," he said.

Overhead, in the curving ceiling of limestone, were dark and tangly weeds. Roots.

"The surface is not far away," said Nixon. "We have been traveling uphill now for a while."

"But what do we do?" I said.

Nixon pulled his hammer from his belt and started digging at the limestone. It crumbled under the hammer's blows. My dad's hunting knife! I pulled the case out of my pocket and removed the knife. The handle was buffalo bone, the blade was iron. The ceiling was only a foot above my head. "Give me that egg, Nixon." I took the wrapped dinosaur egg and placed it on the floor of the tunnel. Then I placed one foot on the egg and braced myself against the wall. I was able to reach the ceiling with my knife. The two of us hacked and gouged and clawed at the limestone.

I fell off the smooth egg a few times. Water continued to gush toward us from the direction of the nesting cavern. Nixon and I were still digging at the soft stone as the water reached my chin.

"Keep digging, Finnegan," said Nixon.

I felt a drop of water. A raindrop. My dad's blade pushed through the limestone. We had reached the surface. A dark hole appeared in the ceiling where my blade had cut. Nixon and I picked at the hole, creating an exit. Outside, the sky was as dark as the tunnel. The water in the tunnel was sloshing against my chin as Nixon hoisted me up with a grunt and pushed me through the hole.

"Finn! Take my egg," he said.

First the egg, then the egg-hound slipped through the hole. Nixon and I sat in wet, dirty sand. Wind and rain howled around us, but we didn't care. I gazed down into the hole, watching the water mere inches from the top. A splash surprised me. The baby crocodile was attempting to climb out of the tunnel. Its small claws were unable to reach the lip of our newly dug hole.

"Oh, all right!" I said. I reached in quickly, grasped the scaly body, and flung the little beast onto the sand. It glanced quickly around, opened and shut its toothy jaws, and then scurried away into a clump of grass.

Nixon Wu stood up and looked around, shielding his eyes from the rain. "The camp is this way," he said.

We ran, but not too quickly because of Nixon's egg and his limp. The Pellagro had burst its banks and was slowly spreading through the dunes on either side. The shrubs, that marked the outline of the camp clearing, were thrashing wildly, but still remained several feet above the angry surface of the river. The wet, spongy grass in the campsite sucked at our shoes. Uncle Stoppard's blue hexagonal tent was blown down. Our car was missing. Where was the portable? Tipped over on the ground. The trailer door was hanging open, banging noisily against the metal side.

Uncle Stoppard and Jared were gone.

20
Buried Gold

"Finnegan!"

Uncle Stoppard hadn't deserted me. And he still hadn't learned how to take down a tent. He was waving at me from inside the collapsed blue hexagon.

"Where did you go, Finn?"

"I was looking for help. For Nixon. What happened to you?"

Uncle Stoppard's clothes were lathered with soap from head to foot. "It's that chemical foam, stuff," he said. "Once we got out, the rain fizzled it all away. That must be how they get the stuff off. With water."

"But how did you get out of the portable?"

"Jared's idea. We rocked it until it tipped over. Then we kicked out the flooring and crawled out."

"But if it tipped over, didn't all the—"

"Yes, and thank goodness that's about the time it started raining."

Uncle Stoppard tripped over one of the metal poles used for framing the tent. "I stayed behind to look for you," he said, crawling to his knees. "Jared busted the trailer door open with a tire iron from the car, and we both got Tulsa and Fleur loose. They drove off in our car to look for Dr. Himmelfarben. Did you find Paz? Hello, Mr. Wu, what's that in your—? Oh, cool. Another egg."

I explained how I found Gabriel Paz on the path.

"Yes, Tulsa told us the doctor killed Paz after we all got loose. I hope they find her," said Uncle Stoppard. "If they don't, I'm sure they'll alert the border guards. Tulsa has his cell phone."

"Do you need some help here, Mr. Sterling?" asked Nixon.

"Oh, no. I've got it all under control, thanks."

"You stayed behind to look for me?" I said.

"Well, uh, yes. I thought I'd get the flashlight from the tent, but that's when it blew over, and I, um, just got out now." He scratched his spiky red hair. "I think I may have been knocked out. Do you see any blood, Finn?"

"No, just more of that foam gunk."

"It'll all probably wash out."

"Let's go find Jared," I said.

"He told us to stay here," said Uncle Stoppard.

I remembered the gun in Dr. Himmelfarben's hand as she aimed it at Uncle Stoppard. "He might need our help," I said.

Uncle Stoppard nodded. The three of us jumped into the Freazes' Jeep and shot down the dirt, I mean, the mud road. "I'd say we drive through Chuca," said Uncle Stoppard. "The doctor probably wanted to avoid Juanpablo."

On the outskirts of Chuca the Jeep bounced violently. We had driven onto the asphalt of the highway. The asphalt turned out to be more slippery than the dirt. And then, about a mile out of town, we almost had another accident. A black car this time, not a truck, barely missed us.

"People drive like maniacs down here," said Uncle Stoppard.

For some reason, I thought that black car looked familiar.

"So Dr. Himmelfarben murdered Professor Freaze?" asked Nixon.

"Yeah, all because of the stupid cacti."

"Cacti?" I said.

"The Giant Golden Finger cacti," said Uncle Stoppard. "Remember we read about it, Finn, in that handbook. A five-thousand-dollar fine if you disturb them. Can anyone find the windshield wipers? Well, each cactus is worth twice that on the black market. And that's what the good doctor was doing. Stealing cacti."

"But how?" I asked.

"With the mechanical Arm," he said. "No, I guess that's the window cleaner. Hmm. It seems that Dr. Himmelfarben needed money as much as the Freazes. She had organized several digs herself and owed lots of people. Because of her knowledge of plants, she was aware of the selling price of the golden cacti. And she knew people back in Arizona that would pay for them."

"I thought she only knew about extinct plants."

"That's what she always said. But as a botanist, she had studied them all. She had been down here a few weeks and started arranging her plans. Oh, *that* button? Thanks, Wu, now I can see much better. Her friends from Arizona had friends down here, the guys in the truck. They got the keys from Dr. Himmelfarben and drove the Arm across the river and into the cactus fields about twice a week. They'd make their trips after everyone had gone to sleep. Each time they came back, they'd carry about four or five cacti in the mechanical Arm's claw."

Four or five golden cacti floating across the ground at night might look pretty spooky to someone who didn't know what was going on. They might even resemble ghosts.

"Then Dr. Himmelfarben would cover them with foam, and the guys would load them onto their truck. They always parked far away from the campsite."

"Why didn't they just drive their truck to the cactus fields?" I asked.

"They didn't want to be caught driving on the highway. Besides, the Arm could approach the *selva del oro* from behind, and they needed the Arm to pull up the cactus, anyway."

"So, why did Professor Freaze have to die?" asked Nixon.

"He didn't sleep well one night. I think it was the Wiener schnitzel. He found out what Himmelfarben was doing and confronted her. Said he was firing her, and that he was reporting her to the cops the next day. I don't think the professor realized how desperately she needed the money."

"So she killed him with the balloon trick?"

"Balloon?" said Nixon.

"I'll explain later," I said.

"The doctor figured people would be so puzzled about how it was done, that they'd never suspect her."

"The bloody cuff!" I said. It was hot that morning. And I suspected Gabriel Paz because he wore a stuffy, uncomfortable tie. But that morning Dr. Himmelfarben was wearing long sleeves. Sleeves for concealing the Mayan knife.

"She took the Mayan knife," I said.

Uncle Stoppard nodded. "That was part of her plan all along. She knew we'd be looking at it early in the morning, and she knew Professor Freaze usually slept later than everyone else. She figured she'd have more time to get the knife. But then Tulsa was looking for the keys to the Arm. And he went and discovered his father a little earlier than the doctor planned. She was still able to get the knife, though, while the rest of us were busy rushing out of the trailer. And she was able to make the switch using an old magician's trick."

"With the handkerchief, I'll bet."

"Exactly. When she grabbed the big handkerchief on the professor's desk, which she already knew was there, she slipped the Mayan knife out of her sleeve. The knife was wrapped inside the folds of the big hankie. When she pulled out the wooden sword, she just had to make a slight twist, and the folds opened to reveal the knife. It looked as if the knife was pulled out of the professor."

"And when she handed the knife and hankie to Jared," I said, "she could slip the sword into her shirt-sleeve."

"Yow! That lightning's bright!" said Uncle Stoppard.

"Oh, Mr. Sterling," said Nixon. "I think we want to stay on the right side of the road."

"I thought we were on the right—oh, yeah."

"How did you figure out about the hankie trick?" I asked.

"I didn't. Himmelfarben explained it herself in the trailer. She was quite proud of her little feat. That's where Jared and I found her, holding the Freazes at gunpoint. Zé's death made things too hot for her, so she decided to vamoose."

"Why kill poor Zé?"

" 'Cause he figured it out," said Uncle Stoppard. "He's the one who noticed the bloody socks on the floor. That's where the doctor concealed the sword."

"What!"

"She didn't want to walk out of the tent carrying the knife. She was afraid people might be searched. So she slipped it through her shirt and her pants down to the floor, and hid it under the socks. She was going to come back for it, but Zé beat her to it. He noticed the blood on the doctor's cuff like you did, Finn. He also noticed the missing radio. Himmelfarben didn't know that Zé had talked with the professor the night before he died. Zé later saw the radio in Dr. Himmelfarben's tent and put two and two together—"

"And was killed?"

"He went to examine the body of the professor the night the Ackerberg people came. Dr. Himmelfarben followed him into the trailer. She saw him comparing the knife wound with the bloody sword. So she reached for the nearest weapon, which turned out to be the dinosaur egg."

Then the doctor must have run to the portable john to throw the sword away, and that's when Tulsa found the door locked. So he stepped inside the trailer and discovered Zé's body.

"Paz was killed out of panic," said Uncle Stoppard. "He had discovered cactus needles scattered throughout the grass of the camp. Remember, plants were one of his specialities, too. He innocently asked the doctor her opinion of them, and that's when she decided to lure him away to the river and kill him. I guess she hoped the storm would wash away the body."

"Look out!" said Nixon. "The bridge is out."

The same rickety bridge that Jared had driven onto several days ago was now collapsed like a cheap lawn chair. "That's our car," I said.

Jared, Tulsa, and Fleur were standing in the rain, by the side of the gorge. Jared waved at us; his blond hair looked brown and droopy in the storm. Outside, the roar of the river was deafening. The once peaceful Pellagro was a fast-moving flood.

"Down there," pointed Tulsa.

The black truck had not been hit by a meteor. But it now lay trapped among the wreckage of the bridge, swallowed by a dinosaur skeleton of metal and wood. Dr. Himmelfarben and a skinny, dark-haired guy were clinging to the roof of the truck.

"What's that stuff?" said Nixon. "Soap?"

Foam spewed out of the truck like lava from a volcano. Dr. Himmelfarben was trapped in a gigantic bubble bath. The chemical spray on the golden cacti was fizzing away in the rain.

"Do you think they'll be okay?" asked Uncle Stoppard.

"As long as that bridge holds out," Jared said. "Hey, there are the cops. Finally."

While Sergeant Diego and his men hauled out ropes and hooks from their car, I whispered something to Uncle Stoppard. "Okay, Finn," he said. "But we better hurry." He got Jared in our car, and then the three of us drove back to the campsite.

Uncle Stoppard's shovel still lay on the ground. But not for long. I didn't care about the rain. I picked up the shovel and started digging in the soft, wet earth.

"Wait a minute, Finn," said Uncle Stoppard.

I noticed the soil under Professor Tuscan Freazes's tent was orange. "What?" I said.

"Clay," said Jared. "This area's already been dug up."

The black car that had passed us on the road. I didn't believe it. I dug as fast as I could, I didn't think about anything else. I didn't see anything except raindrops hitting the wet ground. The soil came up easily. Then my shovel caught on something. An empty plastic bag.

"Uncle Stoppard!" I cried.

"Over here, Finn."

He was pulling a bright object from the folds of our collapsed tent. "Is this what you were looking for?" he said. "I had a little time to dig before I went hunting for my flashlight."

Two feet long, small twinkly eyes, and glistening with rain. It was the golden crocodile, a sly grin curving along its gleaming jaws.

A Note from Stoppard Sterling

Tango dancing, or the *tango,* as it is properly called, originated in Argentina, among the poorer neighborhoods of Buenos Aires. The tango enjoyed worldwide popularity in the 1920s and 1930s, seemed to disappear for a while, and is now being rediscovered around the globe by enthusiastic young people in their twenties and thirties. It is a lively dance for couples. The rhythm is *slow*, slow, *quick*-quick, *slow* and is usually performed with a rose stuck between at least one of the dancer's teeth. (Thornless roses are recommended.)

Dr. Gertrude Himmelfarben, we discovered later, also originated in Argentina. She grew up in one of the wealthier German families that had migrated from Europe at the end of World War II. Dr. Himmelfarben eventually moved to the United States and taught at colleges and universities in Utah, Arizona, and New Mexico. It seems that, like the late Professor Tuscan Freaze, she organized many expeditions which she was unable to afford, and most of her paleobotanical jaunts carried her to Central and South America, where she indulged her twin passions for the plant kingdom and the tango. When Finn discovered the doctor dancing among the dunes, he mistakenly assumed that Gabriel Paz was teaching Dr. Himmelfarben. Actually, the doctor confessed later, she was giving Mr. Paz a few pointers. Paz had known of Gertrude's fancy footwork from Ecuadoran high-society friends, and the doctor was able to use Paz's unspoken yen for the tango to lure him among the lonely dunes. It seems Fleur Freaze also had an unspoken yen: Mr. Paz himself.

As Finn put it so perfectly, who will ever understand adults?

READ THE

FINNEGAN
ZWAKE

MYSTERIES BY MICHAEL DAHL

THE HORIZONTAL MAN
Thirteen-year-old Finnegan Zwake is staying with
his Uncle Stoppard and life is fairly normal—until
the day Finn discovers a dead body in the
basement. It's in the storage area where Finn's
parents left behind gold treasure from their last
archaeological expedition. And missing from the
storage space is a magnificent Mayan gold figure,
the Horiztonal Man....

THE WORM TUNNEL
Finnegan is off to an archeological dig in sunny
Agualar, land of the giant cacti, jungles, and
dinosaurs. Dead ones, that is. While Finn and his
uncle are searching for treasure, the crew is digging
up very valuable dinosaur eggs. But digging too
deeply can stir up trouble, not to mention a murder,
or two, or three....

THE RUBY RAVEN
Finnegan's uncle is invited to be a finalist in an
international mystery writer's award competition.
That means exotic Saharan travel for Finn and
Uncle Stoppard. The winner will receive $1,000,000
and The Ruby Raven, a figurine of a dark, carved
bird, with the real ruby gems as eyes. All of the
writers are eager to win this coveted award, in fact
some are *dying* to possess it....

Available from Archway Paperbacks
Published by Pocket Books

2133-01